Enid Blyton

THE
FAMOUS
FIVE

Everything you ever wanted to know!

Enid Blyton ™

THE
FAMOUS
FIVE

Everything you ever wanted to know!

NORMAN WRIGHT

Illustrations by Eileen Soper

Hodder
Children's
Books

First published in Great Britain in 2000
by Hodder Children's Books

1 3 5 7 9 10 8 6 4 2

For further information on Enid Blyton, please contact **www.blyton.com**

A Catalogue record for this book is available from the British Library

ISBN 0 340 792280 Hardback
ISBN 0 340 792299 Paperback

Text designed by Kim Musselle
Printed in Hong Kong by C&C Offset Printing Co. Ltd

Hodder Children's Books
a division of Hodder Headline Ltd
338 Euston Road
London NW1 3BH

CONTENTS

INTRODUCING THE FAMOUS FIVE

The Famous Five - **Julian**, **Anne**, **Dick**, **George** and **Timmy*** - are amongst the best-loved characters ever to have appeared in stories for children. Mention their names to anyone aged between seven and 70 and they are almost certain to have read one of their thrilling adventures.

By 1942, when Enid Blyton began writing the Famous Five series, she had been a published author for over twenty years and knew exactly the sort of stories her readers loved best. The first book, *Five On A Treasure Island*, contained all the ingredients to make a first-rate holiday adventure. There are golden summer days, a ruined castle, hidden treasure, a sunken galleon and a race against time to save the day. It is an exciting story that carries the reader along a treasure trail at break-neck speed - and for almost sixty years readers have fallen under its magical spell.

As well as introducing the main characters, *Five On A Treasure Island* also made readers familiar with two locations which were to become well-loved by generations of children. These were **Kirrin Cottage**, George's home and the starting off point for many of the Five's adventures, and **Kirrin Island**, the small, rock-bound island sheltering in Kirrin Bay, with its ruined castle, old well and dungeons. These two settings were to feature many times throughout the series.

When Enid Blyton wrote *Five On A Treasure Island*, she intended it to be the first of a series of only six books but, after the sixth story, *Five On Kirrin Island Again*, was published, readers wrote in their thousands demanding more. The same thing happened when she tried to finish the series after twelve books – as Blyton explained in her introduction to *Five Go To*

* names in bold have their own entry within the book

Mystery Moor, the thirteenth book in the series: "in came thousands of letters again. 'But you can't stop at twelve. Please go on forever!' " Blyton hated to disappoint her thousands of loyal Famous Five fans, and she continued to write a new full-length adventure almost every year until 1963, when the twenty-first and final novel, *Five Are Together Again,* was published.

A Famous Five Club for readers was started in September 1952 and profits from the club went to help a children's convalescent home in Beaconsfield, very close to Green Hedges, where Enid Blyton lived. Club members, who numbered well over 200,000, received a special badge depicting the heads of the Famous Five, a membership card, and a letter telling them all about the club and its aims. The club continued for over thirty seven years, finally closing in 1990.

The 21 full-length Famous Five books have remained constantly popular with every generation of children and have never been out of print. Their appeal is the wonderful, timeless world that Enid Blyton created, where there are castles and caves to explore, treasures to find, and mysteries to solve. Along the way there are also interesting characters and animals to meet, not to mention villains to defeat! There are camping trips, boat rides and caravanning holidays and *always* ice-creams, picnics and delicious teas.

The Famous Five books are splendid, fast-moving stories, but part of their success is also due to the original illustrations that went with them. These are by an artist named Eileen Soper, whose pictures add to the books' atmosphere of mystery and adventure and complement Enid Blyton's writing so well.

Eileen Soper was the daughter of the artist George Soper and, from a very early age, drew wonderful pictures. By the time she was fifteen, she had already had paintings exhibited at the Royal Academy. She particularly loved animals and, for most of her life, lived in a big, rambling house with a huge garden which was visited by badgers, foxes, deer and other wild creatures. They became so used to Eileen that she was able to get close enough to draw them. All good research for the Famous Five books, of which she illustrated all 21 novels, as well as many other books written by Enid Blyton, who was a great admirer of her work, writing in 1949: "I don't need to see roughs of *any* of her sketches. She and I have worked together for so long now and I have always found her accurate and most dependable – in fact, excellent in every way..."

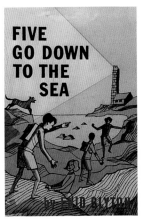

USA Edition

Since Enid Blyton's death, in 1968, the Famous Five books have become even more popular, selling over a million copies a year worldwide. They are published in dozens of countries and have been translated into over twenty languages. There have been Famous Five cinema serials, TV series, and stage plays. The characters have appeared in magazines and comics, on games and on jigsaw puzzles. All over the world there are hundreds of thousands of enthusiasts who read and enjoy the books, always eager to find out more about the stories and all the wonderful characters who appear in them. If you are a Famous Five fan, then this book is for you!

Within these pages you will find all the information on the Famous Five and their world that you could ever want to know. There are sections on the Five, their friends, the villains and animals they come across, the places they visit, and the mysterious castles, caves and passages they explore. Discover some of the real-life locations on which Enid Blyton based **Kirrin Castle**, **Whispering Island**, **Finniston Farm** and other exciting places in the books, take a trip round **Kirrin Village** with the aid of Gillian Clements' wonderful map, or test your knowledge in the quiz section – are <u>you</u> a Famous Five mastermind?

Whatever interests you most, I hope you will enjoy learning more about the Famous Five and their world – as much as I have enjoyed writing about them.

NW

ENID BLYTON
CREATOR OF THE FAMOUS FIVE

Enid Blyton's childhood

Enid Mary Blyton was born on August 11th 1897 in a small flat over a shop in Lordship Lane, East Dulwich, London. When she was only a few months old, the family moved to Beckenham in Kent, an area where Enid and her brothers, Hanly and Carey, spent their childhood. Today Beckenham is a busy town, but a century ago it was a peaceful rural village.

The young Enid was fascinated by natural history and was never happier than when she and her father, Thomas Blyton, went on long nature rambles, where he would point out all the animals, insects, birds and plants that flourished in the fields and woods around their home. Enid's enthusiasm for nature study remained a life-long interest and she later used the knowledge gained as a child in many of her books, stories and articles.

Another of her great loves was reading. She read almost anything that she could lay her hands on, even difficult encyclopaedias! Gradually she began to make up her own stories and poems, which her father encouraged her to write down.

As much as she liked writing stories, she disliked helping around the house and looking after her younger brothers. Her mother, Theresa, shared none of the interests enjoyed by her daughter or husband and, as the years passed, Thomas and Theresa found that they had little in common. Finally, when Enid was in her early teens, Thomas Blyton left home. Enid missed her father very much and never really got over the upset of his leaving.

Thomas had been a keen pianist and had always planned for his daughter to have a musical career but, in 1916, Enid decided that what she really wanted to do was to become a teacher. She telephoned her father, persuaded him to sign the necessary forms and, later in the year, began her training as a primary school teacher. It was in the brief moments of free time she found during her training that she first began to write seriously.

Early poems and stories

At first Enid Blyton could not find a publisher to buy her stories, and for several years her work was constantly returned with rejection slips. However, Enid was determined to succeed, and carried on writing in every spare moment she could find. At last she had a short poem published in a magazine run by Arthur Mee, then another in *Nash's Magazine*.

We do not know what these first two Enid Blyton poems were because both were published without an author's name being given. The first poem published under her name was entitled *Have You....?* and appeared in *Nash's Magazine* in March 1917. A few months later the same magazine published another of her poems, entitled *My Summer Prayer*.

Even when she finished her training and started to teach, Enid still found time to keep writing. In February 1922 she began writing articles for a magazine called *Teachers' World*. At first these were published only occasionally, but from 1929 she wrote a weekly *Enid Blyton's Children's Page*, which usually consisted of a letter, a poem, and a story. She continued to

write regularly for *Teachers' World* until 1945.

Of even greater importance was the publication of her first book, in the summer of 1922. This was called *Child Whispers* and was a short collection of poems. The flimsy, card-covered book had a cover design by Phyllis Chase, a school-friend of Enid's. The book was successful enough for the publisher to issue a further collection, entitled *Real Fairies*, the following year.

Enid Blyton, the author, was on her way!

On to success

In 1924 Enid Blyton married Hugh Pollock, a publisher. By this time her name was becoming quite well-known and larger publishers were beginning to show an interest in her books.

In 1926, Enid and Hugh moved from the flat they had been living in to Elfin Cottage in Beckenham. Soon after the move Enid bought her first family pet, a dog called Bobs, who she described in her autobiography as "a handsome, smooth-haired fox-terrier". Bobs could do many tricks, including sitting up and having a biscuit balanced on his nose, and rolling on to his back when Enid told him to 'die for the King'. He also liked to shut the door and would listen for the 'click' to make sure it was properly closed. When Enid began writing a regular page for *Teachers World,* a '*Letter From Bobs'* was included every week in which Enid, writing as if she were Bobs, would relate everything that had happened to the family during the week. These letters were very amusing and Bobs became almost as well-known to readers as his mistress! Bobs was the first of Enid's many pets to be brought to the attention of thousands of children through her stories and magazine letters.

That same year, Enid also began editing *Sunny Stories for Little Folks*, a fortnightly magazine for younger children. Many of her readers wrote to her and through their letters she gained a good idea of the type of stories they liked to read.

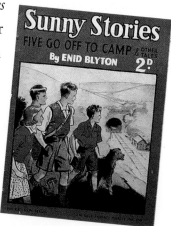

Shortly after starting work on *Sunny Stories*, Enid wrote an adventure story book entitled *The Wonderful Adventure,* about a group of six children searching for a lost treasure. This was Enid's first adventure novel but the firm that published it was so small very few copies were sold. Sadly, this early adventure story was soon forgotten, though Enid continued to write the short stories that were so popular with readers of *Sunny Stories.* Many of these were later collected and published as books.

Another house move came in 1929, when Enid and Hugh moved to Old Thatch, a lovely sixteenth century cottage in Bourne End, Buckinghamshire. This had a much larger garden than Elfin Cottage and gave Enid more space for flowers and pets. It was while at Old Thatch that her two children, Gillian and Imogen, were born – in 1931 and 1935 respectively.

For many years Enid filled *Sunny Stories* with short stories, but when the title of the magazine was changed to *Enid Blyton's Sunny Stories* in 1937, Enid decided to try out a serial story. She called it *Adventures of the Wishing Chair,* and it was so popular with readers that she decided to follow it up with another. This time she thought she would try an adventure story and for issue number 37 she wrote the first episode of *The Secret Island.* The completed story was greeted with great enthusiasm, and was her first full-length adventure story. Soon hundreds of readers were writing in demanding more adventures of Jack, Mike, Peggy and Nora. *The Secret Island* was published in book form in 1938 and a sequel, *The Secret of Spiggy Holes,* started in *Enid Blyton's Sunny Stories* in 1939. Enid knew that children had always enjoyed her short stories but now she saw that her full-length adventures had even more potential. It was time to move on.

Off on an adventure

In 1938, at about the same time as she started to write full-length adventure books, Enid and her family moved house once more. Her daughters were growing up and Enid and Hugh had decided they needed more room. They eventually chose a large house in Beaconsfield. In one of her letters for *Teachers' World*, Enid described the house and its gardens and asked her readers to suggest a name for her new home. Writing in her autobiography many years later, Enid explained how hundreds of children had sent her suggestions – three-quarters of them for the same name: Green Hedges. Enid lived at Green Hedges for the rest of her life and over the years the address became almost as well know as Buckingham Palace and 10 Downing Street.

The move to Green Hedges saw the start of the busiest period of Enid's life. In addition to writing all of the stories for *Sunny Stories* every fortnight and her weekly page for *Teachers' World*, she was also now concentrating on full-length books. She wrote school stories and circus stories but found her adventure and mystery novels were the most popular. But amid all this success there was also sadness, when her marriage to Hugh Pollock ended in 1942, just a few months after the publication of the first Famous Five adventure, *Five On A Treasure Island*.

More adventures and a visit to Toyland

In 1943, Enid married her second husband, Kenneth Darrell Waters, and worked even harder at her writing. The 'Secret' and Famous Five books were becoming so successful that Enid was soon busy writing other series. One of the earliest of these was the 'Adventure' series. The first book, entitled *The Island of Adventure*, was published in 1944. A further seven titles followed. Another popular series was the 'Mystery' series featuring the Five Find-

Outers and Dog, who first appeared in *The Mystery of the Burnt Cottage*, published in 1943. The Find-Outers solved mysteries in and around their home village of Peterswood, a place rather like Bourne End, the village close to Old Thatch.

In March 1949, *The Rockingdown Mystery*, the first book in a series for older children, was published - and later in the same year she wrote the first adventure of The Secret Seven. The Seven had first appeared in a book entitled *The Secret of the Old Mill*, published a year earlier, but *The Secret Seven* was their first 'official' adventure. Soon groups of children all over the country were having meetings, wearing club badges and using passwords just like the Secret Seven! But probably the most crucial event of 1949 for Enid was the publication of *Noddy Goes To Toyland*. Noddy became Enid Blyton's most successful character for very young children and he has remained popular ever since. His adventures have appeared in books and  comics, on television and on the stage - and even in a full-length film. More Noddy toys have been produced over the years than for any other British book character!

How Enid Blyton wrote her stories

Enid Blyton was never happier than when she was writing her stories and books. She was a born storyteller and new plots and characters came easily to her. In her autobiography, *The Story Of My Life*, she told her readers how her stories came about. She never planned them out before starting, but worked completely from "her mind's eye". She would sit down with her typewriter on her knees, then shut her eyes and let her imagination work: "It is almost as if I am looking out of a window, or at a private cinema screen inside my head, and see my characters there - and what I see, I write down."

It was a wonderful gift that allowed her to write a very large number of books and stories. Between January 1940 and December 1949, Enid Blyton had over 200 books published, and during the 1950s this increased to over 300 books! As well as writing all those stories, she also answered hundreds of letters sent in by children, went to book signings and book readings and helped raise money for charity. She also had several hobbies, including playing bridge and golf.

Later days

In the early 1950s, Enid Blyton stopped writing *Sunny Stories* so she could concentrate on a new magazine entitled *Enid Blyton's Magazine*. As well as serialising many of her full-length books and publishing stories about her other creations, including Mr Pink-Whistle and Noddy, the magazine also ran a number of clubs that helped raise money for good causes. The Busy Bee Club raised money for the People's Dispensary for Sick Animals (P.D.S.A.), while the Sunbeams Club helped fund a home for blind babies. Even the Magazine Club itself helped a charity, before the magazine came to an end in late 1959.

During the last few years of her life, Enid Blyton suffered from poor health. The death of her second husband, Kenneth, in 1967, came as a great blow to her and she died a year later on 28th November 1968.

During her lifetime Enid Blyton had been a very private person. Her own autobiography, *The Story of My Life*, written in 1952, was well-illustrated, with many photographs of herself, her home and family, but gave very few details of her life other than her writing. It was not until 1974, when Barbara Stoney wrote *Enid Blyton The Biography,* that the true story of her life was revealed.

In the thirty two years since her death, Enid Blyton's books have remained very popular and continue to sell in huge numbers, both in Britain and the rest of the world. There have been toys, games, television series, magazines, films and stage shows based on her characters. Why *is* her writing so popular? Firstly, and most importantly, she was a born storyteller who knew exactly what children would enjoy. In her stories the world is fresh and green and the days long and sunny. Adults stand back and children do all the things that children love to do: explore secret passages, camp on tree-covered islands, look for lost treasure or roam the countryside in horse-drawn caravans. It is a magical world of make-believe where right always wins and there is always plenty of food and a happy ending. Who could want more?

MEET THE FAMOUS FIVE, THEIR FAMILY AND SPECIAL FRIENDS

Find out all about the main characters as we meet the Five and their friends.

George

Georgina wishes that she were a boy and insists on wearing boys' clothes and having her hair cut very short. She will only answer to the name of George and ignores anyone who calls her Georgina. When Julian, Dick and Anne first meet their cousin they find her a fierce, hot-tempered, lonely little girl. She has blue eyes, short curly hair, a rather sulky mouth and a fierce frown. She enjoys her own company and believes that as long as she has her beloved dog, Timmy, she doesn't need friends. As she gets to know her three cousins she begins to change, gradually realising that things are much more fun when she shares them.

At first George refuses to let her cousins buy her ice-creams. This is because she spends all of her pocket money on food for Timmy, leaving none spare to buy them any in return. But Julian and the others soon persuade her that she has many other things that she *can* share with them, like Timmy, her lovable mongrel dog; Kirrin Island, which her family owns; and Kirrin Castle, the old ruin situated in the middle of the little island.

> George is only persuaded to attend Gaylands School after the Five's first adventure, when Anne, who is already there, explains that pupils are allowed to take their pets with them! Enid Blyton's own school was called St Christopher's, where she excelled at tennis and lacrosse and was made head-girl in her final two years.

By the end of the Five's first adventure, George is a much friendlier person - and her happiness is made complete when her parents finally allow Timmy to stay at Kirrin Cottage for good. She had never been to school when her cousins first meet her but after *Five On A Treasure Island,* she goes to Gaylands School with Anne.

George has many excellent qualities. She has a kind heart, is loyal to her friends and is absolutely truthful. She excels at many outdoor activities and is a wonderful swimmer, rope thrower and climber. She drives the pony and trap kept by the family and can row splendidly, particularly when negotiating the dangerous rocks around Kirrin Island. She has "the sharpest ears of the lot" and we are told "no one had such good eyes as George".

Although she changes for the better after their first adventure, George never loses her hot temper - or her frown - and displays both when she is annoyed or not allowed to have her own way but, as Dick comments in *Five Go Off In A Caravan,* "who can stop George doing what she wants to!"

George is a fearless, determined member of the Five who always plays an important and active part in their exploits. She is held prisoner by villains and kidnapped several times, yet the only time she ever shows any sign of fear is when Timmy is in danger. But crooks and villains had better watch out if they make her angry or threaten Timmy, for sparks are sure to fly before the end of the adventure!

In Enid Blyton's autobiography, there is a chapter entitled 'Which of My Characters Are Real'. In the section on George, Enid says: "Yes, George is real, but she is grown up now." She goes on to explain that the real George was "short haired, freckled, sturdy, and snub-nosed.

She was bold and daring, hot-tempered and loyal. She was sulky, as George is, too, but she isn't now." At the top of the page were two pictures. One from a Famous Five book showing George with Timmy, and the other a photograph of Enid with her dog, Laddie. Enid and George look rather alike in the two illustrations and the description Enid gives of the short-haired, snub-nosed original of George fits reasonably well with what we know of Enid when she was young. In her book, *Enid Blyton The Biography*, Barbara Stoney explains that late in her life Enid "confessed to Rosica Colin, her foreign agent, that George was, in fact, based upon herself."

Julian

Julian is a tall, sturdy, good-looking boy with a determined face and brown eyes. He is the oldest of the Five (twelve years old when we first meet him) and as their adventures progress, considers himself the leader of the group, particularly when they are away from home on one of their many holidays. Indeed, when they are going off on a cycling tour in *Five Get Into Trouble*, Uncle Quentin pays him the compliment of saying "I'd bank on Julian to keep the others in order and see they were all safe and sound." He has good leadership skills, gets on well with people and has a wide general knowledge. Julian is good at finding his way around, having what is described in the books as "a jolly good bump of locality" – which is Enid Blyton's way of saying that he can read a map and use a compass well!

At times Julian tries to be too over-protective and, in *Five Go Off In A Caravan*, even suggests that he should lock Anne and George in their caravan at night for their safety. George won't have it, replying that Timmy is far better protection than any lock.

Though in their early adventures George often appears to be the leader of the Five, as they grow older Julian usually takes command - though George doesn't always accept his leadership without a challenge! In fact, on some occasions, as in *Five Are Together Again*, she totally ignores his 'orders', while Dick jokingly calls him 'Captain', or dismisses his bossiness by telling him that he's beginning to remind him of their headmaster!

Some of the villains the Five come across in their adventures also find that Julian has a very good way with words, and he is known to have a ready tongue when it comes to answering back. The unpleasant **Mr Stick**, who stays at Kirrin Cottage with his equally unpleasant wife while Uncle Quentin takes Aunt Fanny to hospital, thinks that he can keep the Five half-starved and under his thumb. In a battle of words with Julian over the contents of the larder, however, Mr Stick comes out a poor loser. Hunchy at **Owl's Dene** also finds himself at a loss for words when he argues with Julian.

Julian gets on well with responsible adults as he has "a polite, well-mannered way with him that all the grown-ups liked." He is considerate and caring to those in need and always keen to help the police in their efforts to track down the villains the Five regularly encounter.

Dick

Dick is Julian's younger brother and the liveliest member of the Five. At the time of *Five On A Treasure Island*, Dick is eleven years old - the same age as his cousin, George. At the beginning of the story we learn that a few years earlier he had been something of a cry-baby, but has now grown up a lot. He certainly proves himself to be a very resourceful member of the Five throughout their adventures. It is Dick who realises that when George signs 'Georgina' on a note, that it is probably a sign that something is wrong. He also discovers the hidden recess behind the sliding panel at **Kirrin Farmhouse**, and the secret door halfway down the well-shaft on Whispering Island. These lead to two of the Five's greatest adventures.

Dick likes a good joke and can usually see the funny side of a situation. He frequently says things purposely to annoy and niggle George, just so he can see her famous frown! He is good at conjuring and proud of the fact that he is the champion cherry-stone spitter at his school – though he is beaten by **Ragamuffin Jo** when they have a contest in *Five Fall Into Adventure*!

Dick has a number of other skills that he uses throughout the Five's adventures. In *Five Fall Into Adventure* he proves he can speak French fluently, while in *Five Have A Wonderful Time* we find him cooking everyone's breakfast, and demonstrating his boxing skills when he punches the traitorous scientist, **Jeffrey Pottersham**. Although he never demonstrates any first-aid skills, in *Five On Kirrin Island Again* Dick says that he would like to be a doctor when he grows up.

Dick is perhaps best-known for his love of food. All the members of the Famous Five enjoy tucking into a good meal but Dick has a particularly healthy appetite! In their very first adventure we learn that "he was feeling hungry as usual", and in the same story, when the children are listing things they need to take with them on their trip to Kirrin Island, it is Dick who immediately says, "things to eat"!

Food always seems to be delicious and plentiful when the Five are staying on a farm, which prompts Dick to decide, "me for the farm life when I grow up" after he sees - and tastes – the vast spread laid on for them at **Magga Glen Farm** in *Five Get Into A Fix*. When the Five are marooned on Whispering Island with little to eat Anne reminds Dick, "you always take barley-sugars about with you."

Dick is a friendly, reliable, likeable member of the Five who often adds a touch of humour to the stories, yet can be as resourceful and brave as his brother and George when action is needed.

Anne

Anne, the younger sister of Julian and Dick, is ten years old when we first meet her in the opening chapters of *Five On A Treasure Island*. We learn that she likes dolls, enjoys wearing pretty dresses and finds it difficult to control her tongue. In these ways she is quite different to George, her tomboy cousin, yet the two girls soon become inseparable.

Despite their differences, Anne has many of George's qualities. She is loyal, truthful and always prepared to make a personal sacrifice to avoid others missing out on a treat. Despite not always enjoying adventures while they are actually happening – "I'm not a very adventurous person, really" - she is brave and resourceful, and often saves the day with her great puzzle-solving skills. When the Five are snowed-in at Kirrin Cottage, it is Anne who suggests that **The Secret Way** could be used to reach Kirrin Farmhouse in order to search for the missing plans and, when the Five are camping on Kirrin Island, it is she who works out that the Stick family have kidnapped a little girl. Anne also comes up with the idea of going upstream when the Five are trapped in underground passages in *Five Go Off In A Caravan,* and also notices the puzzling fact that although someone has been signalling from the old **Wreckers' Tower** (*Five Go Down To The Sea*), there have not been any recent shipwrecks in the area. She also spots Owl's Hill on the map when the Five are looking for Owl's Dene (*Five Get Into Trouble*) and suggests that the man hiding out in the secret room there is an escaped prisoner. In *Five Go On A Hike Together*, Anne is the one who explains why Dick was given the message meant for **Dirty Dick** in the old barn. Without her the Five would be rather short on brain-power!

Anne is never happier than when the Five are away camping or caravanning and she can organise everything and everybody. She organises the cooking, cleaning and bed-making and ensures that there is always enough food – not an easy job when dealing with five very large appetites! On these occasions she gives the orders and the other three go "obediently to work".

Anne has a quick eye, deft fingers, likes sports and is games captain of her form at school. She enjoys horse riding and it is at her suggestion that she and George go for a holiday at **Captain Johnson**'s Riding School in *Five Go To Mystery Moor*. Another of her interests is looking in second-hand shops. Her favourite colour is red.

Her dislikes include being in very narrow enclosed spaces (such as tunnels and secret passages!), spiders and other creepy-crawlies.

Anne is usually the quietest member of the Five, happy to let one of the others do the talking, but for a time in *Five Have A Mystery To Solve* she turns, as Julian puts it, from a mouse into a tiger. First she throws a bucketful of water over the annoying **Wilfrid** and later, when two men try to take away the children's boat, she and Timmy chase them off.

Timothy

Timmy is found as a puppy by George on the moors and taken home to Kirrin Cottage, where he disgraces himself by chewing up everything in sight. George's father eventually says that the dog must go but, rather than lose him altogether, George gives **Alf**, a local fisherboy, all of her pocket money to look after him for her.

This episode may have had some inspiration from Enid Blyton's own life, as she often told a story of finding a small, bedraggled kitten she named 'Chippy' on the common near her home, and of keeping it secretly until it was discovered and sent away by her parents, who wouldn't let her have pets.

Luckily for George, Timmy isn't banished for long, and at the end of *Five On A Treasure Island,* he is allowed to return to Kirrin Cottage for good. And there he stays, apart from being banished to an outside kennel for a short time after taking a dislike to **Mr Roland**, the tutor in *Five Go Adventuring Again,* so he's always on hand to take part in the Famous Five's adventures.

Timmy grew into "a big brown mongrel dog with an absurdly long tail and a big wide mouth that seemed to grin." When Julian, Dick and Anne first meet him they find him a "friendly, laughable, clumsy creature" and all immediately adore him, despite the fact that his "head is too big, his ears too pricked and his tail too long!"

Timmy is a big, powerful dog and without him to guard them the Five would not have been allowed to go off on their own so frequently. However, it is not an easy life being a dog with such adventurous owners! Timmy loves plenty of walks and is always happy to go wherever the children go but his leg joint gets out of place in *Five On A Hike Together* and on several occasions he has to suffer the indignity of being lowered down into caves and pulled up cliffs with ropes tied round his middle. Almost as bad was the time in *Five Go To Smuggler's Top* when he was lowered down into the **catacombs** in a laundry basket! He is a very clever dog and manages to get himself in and out of all sorts of difficult spots. His most amazing trick was probably the way he got himself up the well-shaft in *Five On A Treasure Island* - how he did it we shall never know!

Even worse than being heaved up and down cliffs on ropes are the times when villains try to poison him, as in *Five Run Away Together, Five Get Into Trouble* and *Five Go Off In A Caravan;* dope him, as in *Five Fall Into Adventure;* hit him with a cudgel, as in *Five Go To Billycock Hill* and *Five Go To Mystery Moor;* or threaten him with guns, as in *Five On A Treasure Island* and several other adventures. In *Five Have A Mystery To Solve* he is actually shot at and loses some fur from the tip of his tail!

When he is not chasing villains or disappearing up secret passages, Timmy enjoys sharing the children's activities. He loves standing in the prow of the boat when the Five row over to Kirrin Island, and enjoys swimming with them in Kirrin Bay. He likes sharing their picnics and agrees with the others that **Joanna** is a wonderful cook. He doesn't like train journeys, ginger beer or mustard but *adores* ice-cream, a word he knows "very well indeed!" But Timmy loves his mistress best of all, and George really is the centre of his world.

Uncle Quentin (Quentin Kirrin)

George's father, and uncle to Anne, Dick and Julian - Quentin Kirrin is a world-renowned scientist who spends most of his time writing learned books, giving lecture tours and working on inventions. One of his most important projects is to discover a new, cheap fuel: "something that will give us heat, light and power for almost nothing." When he is successful he intends to give the results of his work to the world, to benefit the whole of mankind.

He likes to work in peace and flies into a temper if he cannot get the quiet he needs for his work, or if things don't go exactly as he wants them to. Like his daughter, George, he has a fierce frown. We are told that "he and George both looked ugly when they sulked and frowned and both were good to look at when they laughed and smiled."

Uncle Quentin is renowned for being absent-minded. He forgets when the children are due to arrive at Kirrin Cottage for the holidays, forgets to eat his meals, forgets when he is supposed to be going on holiday to Spain and has even been known to put his most important papers in the wastepaper basket by mistake. At the breakfast table he is just as likely to spread mustard on his toast as marmalade!

In the course of his work, Uncle Quentin comes into contact with almost as many villains as the Five. Someone or other always seems to be trying to steal his inventions or the neatly-written notebooks in which he writes all his important formulas. In attempts to make him give up his discoveries he is frequently kidnapped, drugged and knocked out. His safe is robbed and his daughter George held hostage. It really doesn't seem to be an easy life being a scientist!

Aunt Fanny (Fanny Kirrin)

George's mother and aunt to the other three children - Fanny is a gentle, kind woman who tries to keep her clever but impatient husband from finding too much fault with the children. Because Uncle Quentin is so forgetful it is usually left to Aunt Fanny to see to the running of the house. She is particularly cross with her husband for failing to have the ash tree next to Kirrin Cottage trimmed after it crashes down and destroys the roof during a storm.

Fanny's family once owned most of the land around Kirrin Village but over the years it was sold off and, at the time of *Five On A Treasure Island*, only Kirrin Cottage, Kirrin Farmhouse and Kirrin Island remain.

Aunt Fanny is a very good cook and bakes delicious scones and ginger-cake for the children. She is a good organiser and makes sure that there is always a plentiful supply of tinned food in store at the cottage in case they are snowed-in during the winter. The Five use stocks from this store when they run away to Kirrin Island. Fanny also enjoys gardening.

Mr and Mrs Kirrin

We know very little about Julian, Dick and Anne's parents. At the start of *Five On A Treasure Island* we are told that their father is Uncle Quentin's brother, and in *Five Get Into Trouble* we learn that their mother is Aunt Fanny's sister. This must be a case of two brothers marrying two sisters. Further confusion arises when, in *Five Get Into A Fix*, their mother is called "Mrs Barnard", while in several other books in the series Julian refers to them all as "the Kirrins".

In the first story, Julian, Dick, Anne and their parents appear to live close to London, as mention is made of "the crowded London roads" and it takes them a whole day's car journey to reach Kirrin Cottage on the coast. They have a cook and a Welsh gardener named Jenkins. At the time of *Five Go Off In A Caravan* they also have a horse named **Dobby**, used for pulling the pony cart they own. Their doctor, a big burly man who visits the children in *Five Get Into A Fix,* is named Dr Drew.

Later in the series the family seems to have moved much closer to Kirrin Cottage, as in *Five Have A Mystery To Solve* the children not only live on the coast but are only a short cycle ride away from Kirrin.

Mr Kirrin enjoys playing golf and bridge while Mrs Kirrin helps with church sales and bazaars. The couple frequently go abroad for their holidays while Julian, Dick and Anne either stay with George at Kirrin Cottage or go off on an adventure somewhere!

Joanna

Although Joanna, the cook at Kirrin Cottage, is not a relative of the Five she is very much one of the family, appearing or being mentioned in eleven of the 21 Famous Five books. She is a happy, hardworking, jolly woman who has a room of her own in the attic at the top of Kirrin Cottage. She is an early riser, usually up and about by 6.30 a.m. preparing breakfast for the family and starting on the chores for the day.

Timmy was the first of the Five to meet Joanna when he wandered into the kitchen in the opening chapter of *Five Go Adventuring Again*. However, she soon ordered him out, telling him that she knew all about dogs and would not have him wandering about trying to slink off with sausages or anything else! She only permits him into the kitchen once a day, at dinner time. Later in the story, however, when Timmy has been banished to his outside kennel by Uncle Quentin, it is kind-hearted Joanna who takes pity on the dog and brings him into the warm kitchen away from the snow that surrounds his kennel. Despite often complaining about them, Joanna has a very soft spot for animals and is particularly fond of **Mischief**, the monkey owned by **Tinker Hayling**.

Joanna is a wonderful cook who keeps all the family – but particularly the Five – supplied with a continual stream of mouth-watering dinners, puddings and cakes. Dick suggests that Joanna should be given a special award: the OBCBE, which he explains stands for the Order of the Best Cook of the British Empire.

Joanna prepares all sorts of wonderful food for the Five, including scones, ginger cake, sandwiches and potted meat. Perhaps Enid Blyton wrote about food such a lot because at the time of writing the first Famous Five adventures it was war-time and many favourite foods were rationed or unobtainable.

Joanna is away looking after her sick mother during *Five Run Away Together* but returns to Kirrin Cottage at the beginning of *Five On Kirrin Island Again,* when the Five "found Joanna, the old cook there…back to help for the holidays." She is ill for several weeks during their eighth adventure but is back, fully fit and called Joan, at the start of *Five Fall Into Adventure,* a story in which she plays an important part. From then on Joan appears in all the stories set at Kirrin, although at the beginning of *Five Are Together Again* she is taken to hospital suffering from scarlet fever.

Two of Joanna's relatives live close to Kirrin: her sister, who comes to visit her during *Five Have Plenty of Fun,* and her cousin, who lives a bus-ride away. Ragamuffin Jo goes to live with Joanna's cousin in *Five Fall Into Adventure,* after her father is sent to prison.

A TOUR ROUND KIRRIN

You may think you know your way around Kirrin – but do you? Come on a tour of the cottage, island, castle, common and other places around the village where we would all love to live!

Beckton

A fairly large town with a cinema and a town hall, several miles away from Kirrin. It can be reached by road but the Five usually travel there by train.

Coastguard Cottage

Standing on the cliffs overlooking Kirrin Bay and Kirrin Island is the little whitewashed coastguard cottage where the coastguard lives: "a red faced, barrel-shaped man, fond of joking and with an enormous voice." Like almost everyone who lives in Kirrin, the coastguard knows and likes the Five. Whenever they call at his cottage he lets them use his large, powerful telescope to look out to sea and view Kirrin Island. This was particularly useful when Uncle Quentin was staying on the island, conducting one of his experiments, and George wanted to use the telescope to see Timmy, who was staying with him there (*Five On Kirrin Island Again*). The coastguard will often be found in his large shed making wooden toys to sell. Two other cottages stand beside Coastguard Cottage and one of these at least is let out to holidaymakers. Coastguard Cottage can be reached either by a cliff path from Kirrin Cottage or along the road that runs from the back of the cliff to Kirrin Village.

Kirrin Castle

The castle, built of big, white stones, stands on a low hill in the centre of Kirrin Island. It has two towers, one in total ruins and the other in which jackdaws nest. A strong wall once surrounded the castle, but this has long since crumbled away. The entrance is through a great, broken archway

which leads to a flight of uneven steps into the castle yard. The stone slabs that once paved the yard are now broken and covered in sand, blown in from the shore. Where slabs are missing, blackberry and gorse bushes have grown up.

When the Five first went to the island together, looking for lost gold ingots, they cleared many of the bushes from the castle-yard while searching for an entrance to the dungeons. It was Anne who eventually found a stone slab with an iron ring covering the entrance.

The castle dungeons, where prisoners were once kept, are deep underground and are cut into the solid rock. It is dark and damp in the dungeons and noises echo round, making it very eerie. A passage runs under the sea-bed from the dungeons to the old quarry on Kirrin Common.

The old castle well is also in the yard. This was discovered by Timmy by mistake, when he chased a rabbit down a hole and found himself falling through space! Luckily he landed on a slab of stone that had jammed itself partway down the well-shaft. The well-shaft runs down past the dungeons, with a small opening into them. This was used by the Five to escape from the dungeons when they were imprisoned there in *Five On A Treasure Island*.

Only one room in the castle has avoided falling into complete disrepair, and it was in this room, with its two slit windows and a recess where a fireplace had once been, that the Five camped during their first adventure. In *Five On Kirrin Island Again*, George discovered the entrance to under-sea caves and a passage that led under the sea-bed to the mainland from this room.

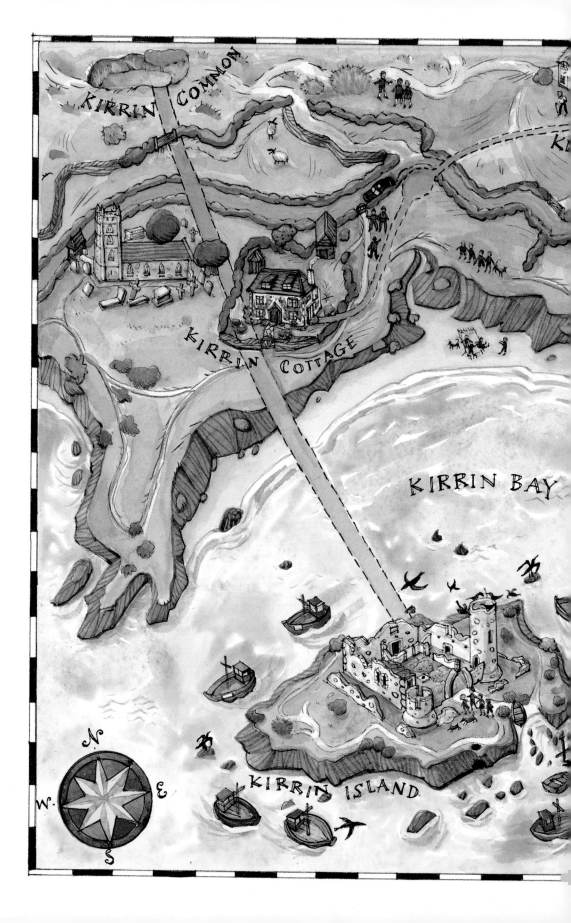

RM

TUNNEL

HEATHER

KIRRIN

PORT
LIMMERSLEY   BECKTON

Kirrin Castle

Kirrin Common

Behind Kirrin Cottage stretches the common, sometimes called the moor. Some areas are lonely and rarely visited and it is in one of these parts that the Five camp in *Five On A Secret Trail*. They travel along Carters Lane and then take one of the winding footpaths over the common, up a hill then down into a little copse, which brings them close to a ruined cottage covered in rambling roses. Near the building is a good spot to camp with a spring, which runs through an age-old channel made of white stone. Close to the spring the Five discover the entrance to a secret passage. Near the ruin is a pool, where the children can swim, and the site of an ancient Roman camp.

Kirrin Cottage

Kirrin Cottage stands on a low cliff overlooking Kirrin Bay with an easy path leading down to the beach. It is not really a cottage at all, but quite a large, old house built over 300 years ago. A crazy-paving path leads up to the porch and the front door. The walls are white stone, but covered with climbing roses and ivy. The ivy is so thick in places that in one adventure Jo climbs up it to look into the girls' bedroom.

Inside the cottage is a sitting room, a dining room and a large kitchen, where Joanna the cook will usually be found baking or preparing a meal. Next to the kitchen is a scullery. At the back of the house, overlooking the garden, is Uncle Quentin's study, where he keeps his important papers and carries out experiments. The Five are rarely allowed into this room, with its panelled walls and stone floor, but one winter's night, George creeps in and discovers the entrance to The Secret Way.

Upstairs the boys share a room with a slanting ceiling and a window that overlooks Kirrin Bay and Kirrin Island. George and Anne share a room with two windows. One of these has a view over the moor at the back of the house, while the other "looked sideways at the sea." In Aunt Fanny's room is a large store-cupboard, packed with tinned food in case of emergency. At the very top of the house is the attic bedroom where Joanna, the cook, sleeps.

In spring the garden is ablaze with colourful flowers: primroses, wallflowers and daffodils. There is a garden shed with two wheelbarrows, a summerhouse, an outhouse for the chickens and somewhere to keep the pony and trap. There are fruit trees in the garden, and a vegetable patch where tomatoes are grown. A giant ash tree once stood close to the cottage but during a storm (*Five Go To Smuggler's Top)* it came crashing down on to the house, destroying the attic, the girls' bedroom and most of the roof.

Kirrin Hill
A hill close to Kirrin Cottage where the Five sometimes go to have a picnic.

Kirrin Island

Nestling in the bay is Kirrin Island, a small, rock-bound island that has been in George's mother's family for generations. In the centre of the island is Kirrin Castle. Deep water and sharp rocks surround the island and only an experienced sailor can steer a boat through them to the little natural harbour. This is a smooth inlet of water running up to a stretch of sand, sheltered between high rocks on the east side of the island. In winter, when the sea is rough and the currents strong, the rocks make it impossible to land on the island or swim out to it.

Kirrin Island is full of wild flowers and large gorse bushes and is home to gulls, cormorants, jackdaws and countless rabbits. Since so few people visit the island, the rabbits are very tame. Timmy finds it almost impossible not to chase them but he knows that this is the one rule that George is *very* strict about. Rabbits are the only things that Timmy and George disagree on!

During *Five On Kirrin Island Again*, Uncle Quentin stays on Kirrin Island to conduct some important experiments and he builds a tall tower to work in.

There is only one cave on Kirrin Island. This was discovered on the seaward side of the island by Dick as the Five made their way back to the beach after clambering over a rocky part of the shore to look at the old wreck. Tall rocks almost completely hide the cave entrance and inside it is perfectly dry as the sea only reaches it during the very worst winter storms. The floor is covered with fine white sand and along one side runs a ledge. In the roof of the cave is an opening that leads out on to the cliff-top. This is hard to find amongst the heather and brambles which criss-cross it, keeping it well-hidden. In *Five Run Away Together,* the Five camped out in the cave – and even captured a prisoner who fell down the hole in the roof!

Kirrin Farmhouse

If the Five are staying at Kirrin Cottage and the sea is too rough for them to row across to Kirrin Island, they will often visit Kirrin Farmhouse to chat with **Mr and Mrs Sanders**, who live there, and explore the secret nooks and crannies of the old farm. It is a pleasant walk to the farm down the lane then along the track that leads across the common behind Kirrin Cottage. The farmhouse is visible from some distance as it stands on a low hill and its white stonework gleams in the sunlight. If it is spring or summer the children usually see some of the farm's sheep grazing in the fields, while Timmy will be on the lookout for the farm's tabby cat. As the Five approach the farmhouse, Ben and Rikky, the two farm dogs, will bark to announce their arrival.

Inside the big, north-facing farmhouse kitchen there is always a warm

welcome from Mrs Sanders. The farm is very old, built in the days when it was sometimes important to be able to hide or escape from enemies, and there are all sorts of hidden cupboards, sliding panels and secret passages. All the downstairs rooms have stone floors and in the hall, close to the majestic grandfather clock, there is a secret sliding panel that opens when the top corner is pressed. Behind the panel is a narrow recess, deep enough to get an arm into but too small even for
Anne to stand in. Mrs Sanders grumbles that every time she dusts she has to be careful or the panel shoots open. In a nook in the wall behind the panel Dick discovered an old book, and Julian, whose longer arm was able to reach in further, found an old tobacco pouch containing the plan of how to find the entrance to The Secret Way. Another hidey-hole can be found in the fireplace where a stone can be pulled up to reveal a space big enough to hide a small box.

Upstairs in one of the bedrooms is a cupboard with a sliding back, which leads to a space big enough for a man to stand in. What had been forgotten over the years was that beyond this is *another* secret door, leading to The Secret Way – it took the Famous Five to re-discover it!

Kirrin Station

The Five usually arrive at Kirrin by train where they are met by Aunt Fanny in the pony and trap. Kirrin Station is a short distance inland from Kirrin Cottage. On foot, the station can be reached by walking across the moors at the back of the cottage. In *Five Run Away Together*, the Five leave a railway timetable open and then set out across the moor to the back of the cottage in order to fool the Stick family into thinking that they are going away by train.

Kirrin Village

Kirrin is a large, thriving seaside village with many shops. These include: an ironmonger's, a hairdresser's, a draper's, a butcher's, a chemist, a bakery, a dairy and a general store. The village has a large hotel (The Rollins) and a garage where Jim, a boy known to the Five, works. In *Five Fall Into Adventure*, we are told that it even has a cinema.

There is a railway station at Kirrin with trains running to the nearby villages of **Seagreen Halt** and **Beckton**. A bus runs down the lane in front of Kirrin Cottage.

There are lovely cliff-top walks from the village offering breathtaking views across Kirrin Bay and over to Kirrin Island. The area inland from Kirrin is fairly hilly with Kirrin Hill close by and Rilling Hill a little further away. A winding lane from the village leads to Windy Cove.

The Old Wreck

For many, many years the old wreck lay in deep water on the far side of Kirrin Island. It was a tall sailing ship that once belonged to Henry John Kirrin, George's great-great-great-grandfather. While he was using it to transport gold bars back to Kirrin Bay, it was sunk in a fierce storm. During *Five On A Treasure Island* another storm drags the wreck up from the sea-bed and sets it down on the jagged rocks that surround the island. The Five are able to explore the old, shellfish-encrusted wreck where they make exciting discoveries. Later, the rough winter seas move the wreck on to rocks closer to Kirrin Island where, at low tide, it can be reached by

clambering over the rocks from the shore.

Port Limmersley

This is the next place along the coast from Kirrin, mentioned in *Five Fall Into Adventure*. It is here that **Red Tower** has his cliff-top hideout, complete with helicopter for quick getaways. The coast between Kirrin and Port Limmersley is very desolate.

The Quarry

About a quarter of a mile across the moors behind Kirrin Cottage is the old quarry. In the past, stone was extracted from it but now it is deserted and, with no footpaths close by, few people visit it. It is shaped like a huge, rough bowl with steep sides. Small bushes, grass and plants grow down its sides and in the spring it is bright with primroses and violets. The Five sometimes go to the quarry searching for flint arrow-heads, and enjoy a picnic there sheltered from the wind. Timmy made an exciting discovery while digging for rabbits in the quarry.

Seagreen Halt

A tiny village between Kirrin and Beckton. There is a small railway station here and a few cottages. It is in one of these cottages that a valuable Pekinese dog, stolen from the dog show in Beckton, is being hidden in the short story entitled *Five And A Half-Term Adventure,* published in *Five Have A Puzzling Time And Other Stories.*

Uncle Quentin's Tower

For one of his scientific investigations, Uncle Quentin needs a place where he has water all around him. He takes all of his equipment to Kirrin Island and has a strange tower built in the castle yard. It looks rather like a lighthouse but is made in sections from some smooth, shiny material, that Julian guesses is a kind of plastic. At the top of this tower is a room with walls of thick glass. A narrow spiral staircase leads up to it. Wires run right through the glass and their free ends wave and glitter in the wind. When Quentin is experimenting, the wires activate by some secret power and light up. Quentin Kirrin's experiments here are very important in his quest to develop a new fuel to replace coal, coke and oil.

WHERE WAS KIRRIN CASTLE?
AND OTHER LOCATIONS IN THE FAMOUS FIVE BOOKS

You will not find Kirrin or Kirrin Island on any map of Great Britain but Enid Blyton did base these and other places mentioned in the Famous Five books on actual places she had seen, visited or heard about. As she wrote in a letter to a psychologist in 1953: "There are...many islands in my stories, many old castles, many caves - all things that have attracted me in my travels. These things come up time and again in my stories, changed, sometimes almost unrecognisable - and then I see a detail that makes me say - yes - that's one of the Cheddar Caves, surely!" Read on to find out more about some of these 'real life' locations!

Billycock Caves

In *Five Go To Billycock Hill*, the children visit the Billycock Caves. Here they see some wonderful displays of stalactites and stalagmites, including rainbow-coloured formations, and groups that are so close together that they have formed a "snow-white screen". Julian says that the great chamber they come to within the caves reminds him of a cathedral. There is only one place in the country that matches this description - the famous caves at Cheddar Gorge in the Mendip Hills, where it is possible to see beautiful stalactite and stalagmite formations similar to those seen by the Five. These caves are open to the public.

Castaway

The town of Castaway in *Five Go To Smuggler's Top* is built on top of a hill surrounded by an ancient wall, with one road into the town still running through an original gateway arch. This is very like the beautiful East Sussex town of Rye, which, like Castaway, still has cobbled streets and many shops with diamond-paned windows. Castaway is surrounded by treacherous

marshes, as Rye once was centuries ago, and the land around the rocky hill on which Rye is built is still very low lying and liable to flood. Rye, like Castaway, also has a traditional history of smuggling and in past ages characters like Mr Barling would have been very much at home there, carrying on a brisk trade in smuggled goods. Unfortunately, unlike Castaway, the hill upon which Rye is built is *not* honeycombed with secret passages!

Finniston Farm

In a 'Special Note from Enid Blyton' at the start of *Five On Finniston Farm,* Enid tells her readers that Finniston Farm is "a real farm in Dorset", owned by her family. She goes on to say that the old chapel is still there and that the great Norman door described in the story is also still to be found at the entrance to the kitchen. This 'real farm' was, in fact, Manor Farm at Stourton Caundle, near Sturminster Newton in Dorset, which Enid and

her husband bought in 1956. Enid never actually lived at Manor Farm but as she loved Dorset and was frequently on golfing holidays in the area she had plenty of opportunity to visit and help plan how it was run. Enid mentioned her farm and the animals on it several times in *Enid Blyton's Magazine,* though it was sold in 1962. It is now in private hands and not open to the public.

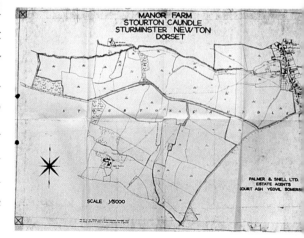

Kirrin Castle

The first clue to where we might find Kirrin Castle comes in Enid Blyton's *Children's Page* letter, published in *Teachers' World* on 20th May 1931, where she writes about a castle she has visited: "As I drove along in my little car I saw, far away in the distance, a rounded hill, and on it was the ruin of an old, old castle." She goes on to tell her readers that at first she thought the castle looked lonely until she saw that hundreds of jackdaws nested in the ruins and rabbits – so tame that they popped out of their holes and frisked right up to her – played in the deserted courtyard. She does not mention the name of the castle but a photograph printed with the letter shows it to be Corfe Castle in Dorset. Could this be the castle that gave Enid the idea for Kirrin Castle?

The answer to this question is probably yes, as Enid loved the county of Dorset and often spent holidays in Swanage, the seaside town about ten miles from Corfe. On her visits to Swanage she would have passed the imposing ruined tower of Corfe Castle several times.

There are many similarities between Corfe and Kirrin. They are both built of white stone and both have only one large tower still standing, as well as a big arched entrance to the inner part of the castle. At Corfe this huge archway has a great break across it and one side has slipped downwards several metres. When the Five first go to Kirrin Castle we are told that they "gazed at the enormous old archway, now half broken down." Both Kirrin and Corfe have jackdaws nesting in their towers and, although the chances of seeing rabbits running around the courtyard at Corfe these days are slight, when Enid first visited the castle it had few visitors and would have been well-suited to rabbits.

Corfe Castle is now owned by the National Trust and can be visited on most days of the year. It has a magical feel and I have no doubt that Enid Blyton used it as her model for Kirrin.

Kirrin Island

In the Famous Five stories, Kirrin Castle is, of course, built on an island but, though Corfe Castle is situated in an area known as The Isle of Purbeck, it is not really an island at all, but a peninsula with the sea ten miles away. So where did Enid Blyton get her inspiration for Kirrin Island from? Some people have suggested it is based on Brownsea Island in Poole Harbour, but Enid did not visit Brownsea until several years after *Five On A Treasure Island* was published. The real answer to the Kirrin Island question was, however, finally cleared up by Trevor Bolton in an article for the *Enid Blyton Society Journal*.

Trevor corresponded with Enid from 1948 until the early 1960s and in his letters he often asked questions about her books and stories. In one letter he asked her if Kirrin was based on a real place and in her reply she said: "Yes. Kirrin was based on an actual village, bay and island – but in the Channel Isles, not England." Enid Blyton visited Jersey during her honeymoon in 1924 and, if not based on Jersey itself, it is likely that Kirrin Island was inspired by one of the many small isles she visited nearby.

Whispering Island

In a 'Special Note from Enid Blyton' at the beginning of *Five Have A Mystery To Solve,* Enid explains that Whispering Island is based upon an actual island in a "great blue harbour" and that the golf course and **Hill Cottage** mentioned in the story can both be found overlooking that same harbour.

The great harbour mentioned in Enid's story as "a wonderful harbour" and described by **Mrs Layman**, who lives at Hill Cottage, as "the second biggest in the whole world" is Poole Harbour, one of the largest natural harbours in the world, while Whispering Island is based on Brownsea Island, the largest of the five islands in Poole Harbour.

Brownsea now belongs to the National Trust and a large part of it is a nature reserve. Many trees cover the island and, as in the story, the wind continually blowing through them does make a whispering noise. The island also has a castle, known as either Brownsea or Branksea Castle, rebuilt during the 18th century, but this is not open to the public. Ferry boats run to the island from Poole Quay and for a small landing charge it is possible to walk round the nature trail. Although you will not find the old well or any of the mysterious statues described in *Five Have A Mystery To Solve*, you might be lucky enough to see some of the red squirrels that still inhabit the island. Dogs are not allowed on Brownsea, however – so if the Five visited again poor old Timmy would have to stay at home!

The golf course mentioned in the story is still there, set in Studland Bay and overlooking Poole Harbour. Enid Blyton and her husband, Kenneth, bought it in 1951, and usually spent several holidays a year in the area. Enid gives a very full description of Hill Cottage but I have never managed to find it. Perhaps *you* will have more luck if you visit Studland!

Faynights Castle

Faynights Castle, visited by the Five in *Five Have A Wonderful Time,* is set on a high hill several miles from the coast and has one remaining tower with the rest in ruins. Part of its surrounding wall has fallen down the hill and lies half-buried in grass and weeds. This description is very much like that of Corfe Castle, mentioned earlier as Enid Blyton's model for Kirrin Castle, and it is quite possible that Enid used Corfe as a model for both her fictional castles. Certainly Eileen Soper's illustrations depict Faynights Castle looking very like Corfe.

FRIENDS AND ALLIES

While adventuring, the Five encounter many friendly and helpful people - see if you can find your favourites in this chapter! (NB: the number of the Famous Five book in which the character appears is listed in brackets.)

Aggie (8) When the Five are prisoners at Owl's Dene they find a friend in Aggie, the down-trodden housekeeper of **Mr Perton**. Aggie has a miserable life, made worse by the bad-temper of her brother, Hunchy. The children are friendly towards Aggie and in return she sees that they have plenty of food. She warns them that Hunchy plans to poison Timmy.

Alf (1+) One of George's few friends before *Five On A Treasure Island*, Alf is the fisher-boy who looks after Timmy when Uncle Quentin forbids George to keep him at Kirrin Cottage. Alf is about fourteen years old with a ready grin and tousled hair. He is adored by Timmy and is one of a number of fishermen who look after George's boat for her. He also appears as James, mending the broken rowlock in *Five Have Plenty Of Fun*, and Jim, painting the boat in *Five Run Away Together*.

Alfredo the fire-eater (11): One of the fair folk who camp in the same field as the Five near Faynights Castle. He is "a great big fellow with a lion-like mane of tawny hair", yet is continually bossed around by his tiny wife. Alfredo is Ragamuffin Jo's uncle and it is her arrival at Faynights Field which stops the Five from leaving after the fair folk are hostile towards them.

Aily (17) The small, wild-looking girl who roams the Welsh mountains dressed only in ragged shorts and blouse, seemingly oblivious to the cold. Aily, with her "face as brown as an oak apple", wanders the mountainside with her lamb, **Fany**, and her dog, Dave, singing in her "high, sweet voice". At first she is nervous of the Five but their kindness reassures her and she is soon treating Julian like an elder brother. Aily cannot read but she has a wonderful sense of direction and shows the Five how to get into **Old Towers** where they believe Bronwen Thomas is being held prisoner.

Jennifer Mary Armstrong (3): Jennifer Armstrong – known as Jenny – is a little girl kidnapped by the Stick family and held prisoner on Kirrin Island. Despite her young age she shows great courage when the Five rescue her from the dungeons of Kirrin Castle and wants to stay with them on the island when the adventure is over. Like Anne she loves dolls – she owns four, called Josephine, Angela, Rosebud and Marigold. Jenny is a small girl with large dark eyes and dark red hair that tumbles over her cheeks. She lives close to the sea with her parents. Her father, Harry Armstrong, is a millionaire and a ransom of £100,000 was demanded for her safe return.

The Barnies (12): A group of travelling players who give theatrical performances to villagers in Cornwall. Their repertoire includes singing, dancing, fiddle playing and the hilarious performance of **Clopper**, "the funniest horse in the world". At each stop they clear a barn, build a stage of planks supported on barrels, set up their home-painted scenery and give a number of evening performances. Their boss is the **Guv'nor**, who uses the Barnies' theatrical activities as a cover for smuggling.

Ben the blacksmith (13): A big, eighty-year-old blacksmith with a mane of white hair, who has lived close to **Mystery Moor** all his life. He only appears once in the story but tells the children the tale of the Bartles and how Mystery Moor got its name.

Jeremiah Boogle (19): An old sea-man who now spends most of his time on the quay at **Demon's Rocks** smoking his pipe and telling stories of the 'old days' to anyone who will listen. It is Jeremiah who tells the Five and

 Tinker of the wreckers who once operated around the coast near Demon's Rocks and of the treasure that One-Ear Bill is supposed to have hidden. Jeremiah also shows the children the **Wreckers' Cave**. The old man later helps to free the Five and Tinker from the lighthouse when they are locked in by **Ebenezer and Jacob Loomer**.

 Martin Curton (6): A quiet, sulky boy of about sixteen who comes to stay with his guardian at the cottage next to the coastguard. He is a talented painter and helps the coastguard by painting some of his wooden toys, though his guardian disapproves of this. Martin has had a miserable life, his mother is dead and we do not know what has happened to his father. His guardian, **Mr Curton**, is a crook mixed up in all kinds of dishonest schemes. After Mr Curton is taken away by the police, Martin goes to stay with the coastguard and Uncle Quentin promises to help him get into art school.

 **Fair folk (11):** In *Five Have A Wonderful Time*, a number of the fair folk help the Five when they are held captive in the tower room at Faynights Castle. These include Mr Slither the snake man, Bufflo the whip expert (pictured) and his wife, Skippy, and Jekky the rope man.

Mr Gaston (10): A wealthy man who lives at Spiggy House close to Beacons Village on the moor. Mr Gaston owns a number of horses and is something of an amateur vet. When Timmy hurts himself climbing down a rabbit hole, Mr Gaston is able to put it right. Later, when the Five have successfully found a large quantity of stolen jewels, it is Mr Gaston whom they telephone for help. He comes in his car to fetch them and takes them to see the police inspector at Gathercombe, where they not only hand over the jewels but are also given the chance to wash and change before going back to school.

Grandad (12): **Yan's** great-grandad is over ninety but still lives in a tiny shepherd's hut and works as a shepherd on **Tremannon Farm**. He isn't very big, seems shrivelled like an over-stored apple and has a face with a thousand wrinkles. His hair and beard are as grey as the sheep he tends. He tells the Five of the **Wreckers' Tower** where, almost a century before, his father lit a false light on stormy nights to lure ships to their destruction and says that on wild nights the light still shines from the tower. Grandad goes to the show given by the Barnies and thoroughly enjoys it, but tells everyone that he is only there for the slap-up supper that follows the performance!

Great-Grandad (18): See **Jonathan Philpot**.

The Harries - Henry and Harriet Philpot (18): Despite one being a girl and the other a boy, Henry and Harriet look identical. Once the twins have made friends with the Five they let them on the secret of how to tell them apart: Harry has a scar on his hand where he once cut it on barbed wire.

Professor Hayling (19/21): The scientist father of Tinker and even more forgetful than Uncle Quentin! He forgets his meals, leaves papers in the wrong place and never remembers when he has asked people round to visit. He keeps his most important papers in a tower built in his garden. The professor smokes a pipe and has a tremendous laugh.

Henry (Henrietta) (13): A tomboy of about the same age and build as George. Henry is wiry and strong, has a broad grin and is an excellent rider. She likes to stride about in her riding jodhpurs, whistling. She has three brothers, and two great-aunts who fuss over her. George is jealous of Henry and is annoyed when Julian and Dick mistake her for a real boy! The two girls gradually become friends and when Anne and George are held captive on Mystery Moor, Henry plays a big part in their rescue.

Jenny (21): The long-suffering maid of Professor Hayling at **Big Hollow**

House. Jenny is a wonderful cook, with a character similar to that of Joanna, the cook at Kirrin Cottage. She has quick ears and hears the quiet noises made the night Professor Hayling's secret papers are stolen. She feels the cold and does not like swimming.

Jo (9/11/14): See **Ragamuffin Jo.**

Captain Johnson (13): Has been the owner of a riding school near Milling Green for fifteen years. He is a burly, hot-tempered man who stands no nonsense from anyone. He runs riding holidays for boys and girls with his wife, where he works the children hard but they enjoy every minute of it. He has a reputation for knowing all about horses, with even the gypsies taking their horses to him if they are unwell.

Morgan Jones (17): The giant farmer of Magga Glen has a powerful voice but actually says very little – except when communicating with his seven working dogs! Morgan has a mass of black hair, bright blue eyes and a stern mouth. He seems to have the strength of half-a-dozen horses.

Richard Kent (8): The Five first encounter Richard when they are camping close to the Green Pool, a small lake owned by Richard's millionaire father. He is a well-built twelve-year-old with fair hair, blue eyes and a rather boastful manner. Richard is keen to go part of the way with the Five on their cycling tour and later lies to them that he has permission from his mother to cycle with them as far as Great Giddings, where his aunt lives. Richard is rather a spoilt child. He has a cowardly nature and seems to think only of his own safety. He is easily scared and bursts into tears when the slightest danger threatens. Julian at first thinks that he is "too feeble for words" but, as the story progresses, Richard begins to see some of his faults and by the end of the adventure he has changed for the better, thanks to the good influence of the Five.

Guy and Harry Lawdler (15): The twin sons of archaeologist and explorer Sir John Lawdler, both boys take after their father and enjoy excavating Roman remains. When the Five first meet the boys on Kirrin Common they do not realise that there are two of them and continually talk at cross purposes before they realise that they are dealing with twins! Guy, who owns **Jet**, the little mongrel dog, enjoys joking and tricking, while Harry prefers reading.

Mrs Layman (20): "A cheerful smiling old lady" who lives "up on the hills overlooking the harbour". She has known the Kirrin family for a very long time and is best remembered by the children for never forgetting their birthdays! She wants the Five to go and stay at **Hill Cottage** for a few weeks to keep her grandson, **Wilfrid**, company.

Marybelle Lenoir (4): Marybelle is a small girl of Anne's age. She is a pale and delicate child with golden hair and blue eyes. She is naturally shy but gets on well with the Five and joins in the adventure that takes place at her home, **Smuggler's Top**. Her half-brother, Pierre, who is as dark as she is fair, jokes that they are like 'beauty and the beast'.

Mr and Mrs Lenoir (4): Marybelle's father and Pierre's step-father, Mr Lenoir (pictured) has fair hair, a deep voice and cold eyes and seems full of secrets. The children don't know what to make of him when they first meet and for a long time believe that he is involved in smuggling. He has very fast mood changes – one minute he is laughing and telling jokes and the next he is in a fierce temper – but the children always know when he is about to explode as the tip of his nose goes white. He detests dogs and will not have them in the house, which makes things rather difficult when George takes Timmy along with her to stay at his home, Smuggler's Top. Mr Lenoir hopes to work with Uncle Quentin to drain the marshes surrounding his house and sell the reclaimed land for development.

Mrs Lenoir is timid like her daughter and, as Anne points out, has the smallest hands she has ever seen on an adult. She seems to be scared of her husband and dislikes living at Smuggler's Top. At the end of *Five Go To Smuggler's Top* she is pleased when her husband tells her that as she is unhappy there they will move.

Pierre Lenoir (4): Pierre goes to the same school as Julian and Dick and is, according to the boys, as mad as a hatter and always ready to play a practical joke. He climbs like a cat, can be very cheeky and at school has the reputation of never doing as he is told. Probably his most outrageous antic was to saw halfway through his form-master's chair-leg. We never learn what happened when the teacher sat on the chair!

Pierre lives with his mother, step-father and half-sister at Smuggler's Top and is a lively and entertaining host when the Five go to stay with him while Kirrin Cottage is having its roof mended. Pierre has very dark hair, eyes like bits of coal and black eyebrows. He has the nickname 'Sooty' and explains that Lenoir is French for 'the black one'. He is a bit of an inventor and rigs up a buzzer that sounds when anyone approaches his room. With his dancing eyes and wicked grin he is immediately liked by the Five. He is also one of those people whom dogs naturally like. As he tells George, he could box her ears and Timmy would still lick his hand! As would be expected from such a character, Pierre is a great explorer and knows every inch of the house and town where he lives.

Bobby Loman (Short stories): An orphan aged about eleven who lives in Kirrin Village with his grandfather. Bobby has two pets: **Chippy**, a mischievous little monkey, and **Chummy**, a cross-breed Alsatian dog. When Chummy bites someone, and his grandfather threatens to have the dog destroyed, Bobby runs away to Kirrin Island. The Five find him there and persuade him to return to Kirrin Cottage with them. The problem is resolved when his grandfather says he will have the dog properly trained.

Lucas (20): Once one of the 'watchmen' on Whispering Island, Lucas is

now a groundsman working on the golf course close to Hill Cottage. He has dark, deep-set eyes and an extremely tanned face, shoulders and arms from continually working out of doors. Timmy adores him and the Five find him friendly and easy-going. He is a born story-teller and holds the children enthralled with the strange history of Whispering Island.

Mr Luffy (7): A teacher at the boys' school and a friend of the family who often plays cards with Julian's parents, Mr Luffy has a passion for studying insects and is known by the boys at his school for being absent-minded, yet fun. He is untidy with thick hair, shaggy eyebrows, gentle brown eyes and an untidy moustache. He can waggle his right ear and this is a party trick that everyone, particularly Anne, enjoys seeing him do. He takes the Five off on a camping holiday but is thoughtful enough not to interfere with their plans or be too inquisitive about what they are up to. Mr Luffy takes **Jock Robbin**'s side when **Mr Andrews** wants Jock to return to **Olly's Farm** instead of camping with the Five. Mr Luffy is not a very good driver but he is an excellent swimmer.

Nobby (5): We never learn Nobby's surname but we do know that he is an orphan and that his father was a clown at Mr Gorgio's circus. He is about fourteen years old, has a freckled face and his favourite expression is "Jumping Jiminy". He first meets the Five as the circus procession passes Julian, Dick and Anne's home and, after chatting with him, the children decide to go on a caravanning holiday to the **Merran Hills** where the circus is camping. Nobby has a great way with animals and hopes that one day he can work with horses. His best friends at the circus are his two dogs, **Barker** and **Growler**, and **Pongo** the chimpanzee. Nobby has never been to school and can only read a little. He gets on well with the Five and enjoys sharing their picnics and their adventures. He is delighted when Farmer Mackie gives him a job working with the farm horses.

Old Grandad (21): See **Mr Tapper**.

Mr Penruthlan (12): The Cornish farmer of **Tremannon Farm**. A big, broadly-built man over six feet tall, he is darkly sunburnt with black eyes, a mane of black, curly hair and huge hairy hands. He has a big appetite and spends a lot of time without his false teeth, which makes it impossible for anyone except his wife to understand what he's saying! At first the Five believe him to be a smuggler but they eventually discover he is working with the police to track down the real smugglers.

 Mrs Penruthlan (12): Wife of Mr Penruthlan and mother of seven children, now all grown up. She is a "plump little woman", and one of the best cooks the Five have ever known. She enjoys nothing better than spending the entire day cooking and preparing food for a party or harvest celebration.

 **Jonathan Philpot (18):** Known by all as 'Great-Grandad' and now getting on for ninety years of age, old Jonathan still does a full day's work around **Finniston Farm**. He has "a shock of snowy white hair, a luxurious white beard reaching almost to his waist and very bright eyes". When he's not working on the farm he's usually sitting in his big chair in the dining room. He has a loud voice which he uses to great effect when he dislikes something. His great friend is William Finniston, who is a descendent of the original builder of the castle that once stood close to Finniston Farm, as well as the owner of a small antique shop in Finniston Village.

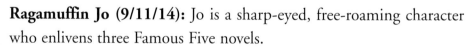 **Ragamuffin Jo (9/11/14):** Jo is a sharp-eyed, free-roaming character who enlivens three Famous Five novels.

When she first appears in *Five Fall Into Adventure,* dressed in dirty shorts and a filthy jumper and with her "short curly hair, brown freckled face and fierce expression", Julian, Dick, George and Anne think that she is a boy. Jo leads a very uncertain life as her mother, who worked in a circus training dogs, died when she was very young, and her father, who was once an acrobat, injured his foot and can no longer work. The pair now live in a caravan making a living as best they can.

Jo has a wonderful way with animals and Timmy immediately goes to her when she calls him, though the rest of the Five mistrust her on their first meeting and they have a number of disagreements. When they later find out that it was Jo who gave Timmy doped food and assisted in George's kidnapping, their feelings towards her turn to disgust.

Jo eventually redeems herself by helping Julian and the others to find George. Although she is unable to read and write properly in *Five Fall Into Adventure*, Jo does have some wonderful skills. She is a marvel at tracking and can unerringly find her way about the countryside without the aid of a map or compass. She can climb almost any wall and gives Anne a fright one evening when she swarms up the ivy-covered wall of Kirrin Cottage and peers in at her bedroom window! At the end of her first adventure with the Five, Jo goes to live with Joanna's cousin, who lives a bus ride away from Kirrin.

We next meet Jo in *Five Have A Wonderful Time*, when she is visiting her uncle, Alfredo, a fire-eater in a circus, at Faynights Field. She arrives just in time to prevent a disagreement between the Five and the fair folk and then finds herself involved in an adventure, where she makes friends with a pair of pythons and once again finds her climbing skills very useful.

Jo's final adventure with the Five is in *Five Have Plenty Of Fun*. She is now leading a more settled life, living with Joanna's cousin and going to school regularly, but she is still the "scamp and scallywag" that she has always been. In this adventure Jo helps Julian, Dick and Anne to discover where kidnappers are holding George.

 **Jock Robins (7):** A good-tempered boy of about twelve who lives with his mother and step-father at Olly's Farm on the **High Moors**. He has straw-coloured hair, blue eyes and a rather red face. Before the death of his real father he lived on Owl's Farm. Jock has never had an adventure before and is very excited at sharing one with the Five.

'Wooden Leg' Sam (7): The grey-whiskered watchman who looks after Olly's Yard. Has difficulty seeing what is going on since he "bruck his glasses". He tells the Five of the spook train and tells them to keep away from the yard and the railway.

Mr and Mrs Sanders (2): Mr and Mrs Sanders of Kirrin Farm do not have any children of their own and are always pleased to see the Five when they visit. Mr Sanders, who is going rather deaf, likes to remind George that he and his wife have known her *and* her mother since they were babies. Mrs Sanders, whose great-grandmother, Alice Mary Sanders, also lived at the farm, is a small, lively woman usually to be found working in the warm farmhouse kitchen. She enjoys nothing better than baking cakes and biscuits and Mr Wilton, one of the artists staying at the farm during *Five Go Adventuring Again,* thinks that she is a wonderful cook - the Five agree and are always eager to try one of her homemade cakes or biscuits! Mrs Sanders is delighted when Dick discovers her great-grandmother's old recipe book in a recess behind a sliding panel in the hall.

The farm, which seems to consist mainly of sheep and poultry, does not make a lot of money and to help out Mrs Sanders takes in paying guests. At Christmas Mr Sanders always sends a fine turkey to Kirrin Cottage.

Constable Sharp (19): The hefty policeman at Demon's Rocks who helps the Five to recover some of their stolen property and also assists with their rescue when they are imprisoned in **Demon's Rocks Lighthouse**. Unlike some of the policemen the Five encounter, PC Sharp is very helpful and seems to know exactly what goes on in his village.

Sid (9): The newspaper delivery boy who calls at Kirrin Cottage and once spent the evening with the children while Dick took his place in order to keep a lookout for villains!

Sniffer (13): A thin, wiry, little fellow who leads a miserable life with his father, aunt and grandma. His life is made bearable by his love for his dog, **Liz**, and the caravan horse, **Clip**. Sniffer is so called because of his habit of continually sniffing. Even when George gives him a large red-and-white striped handkerchief to blow his nose with, he prefers to keep it clean and neatly folded rather than use it! Sniffer has plenty of courage and stands up to his father several times in an effort to help the Five. His dream is to live in a house and own a bicycle. After he helps George and Anne escape from captivity, George promises that she will buy him a bike.

Sooty (4): See **Pierre Lenoir**.

Spiky (14): A "short plump boy with a pleasant lop-sided face… eyes as black as currants… and a mop of black hair which sticks up into curious spikes." He works at **Gringo**'s fair and gives the children a lead after George is kidnapped.

Mr Tapper (21): Owner of the circus that has the right to camp at Cromwell's Corner field once every ten years. Also known as Old Grandad, Mr Tapper is rather fierce-looking, with a long, bushy beard, enormous eyebrows and only one ear. He has a deep voice but is really a very friendly character. His family have been travelling players since Norman times and he is a favourite with the circus monkeys.

Jeremy Tapper (21): The ten-year-old grandson of Mr Tapper. Like all of the Tappers, Jeremy will never give in when arguing, which leads to a fight with Tinker. Later the two boys shake hands and become friends.

Derek Terry-Kane (11): A scientist, known to Uncle Quentin, who disappears and is discovered by the Five in Faynights Castle where he is being held prisoner by **Jeffrey Pottersham**. He has "big, thick, arched eyebrows, and (an) enormous forehead."

Benny Thomas (16): Younger brother of **Toby Thomas**, and keeper of strange pets - the latest of which is a piglet named **Curly**. Benny has yellow curly hair, fat little legs, brown eyes and a high voice. His favourite phrase, when speaking of Curly, is that "he runned away." Benny uses this as an excuse for wandering away from the farmyard. His previous pets included a lamb and two goslings.

 Jeff Thomas (16): Jeff is a Flight Lieutenant at the Billycock Hill Air Force base, where he flies one of the experimental fighter planes. He is a tall, strong, good-looking young man with "eyes as keen as hawks". When two planes go missing from the base, he and his friend, fellow pilot Ray Wells, are suspected of being traitors.

 Toby Thomas (16): Julian and Dick's school-mate who lives on Billycock Farm and arranges the camping equipment and food when the Five go to Billycock Hill. Toby is a bit of a joker who enjoys putting caterpillars down people's necks and drenching his school friends with water-squirting imitation roses. During the school holidays he works hard at jobs around the farm including milking cows, cleaning out sheds, collecting eggs and even whitewashing out-houses. His cousin, Jeff Thomas, is his great hero.

 Tinker (19/21): The nine-year-old son of Professor Hayling, who comes to stay at Kirrin Cottage with his pet monkey, Mischief, while his father and George's discuss important work. Tinker is obsessed with cars and spends most of his time running around imitating the noise of a car or lorry engine. When the noise of all the children and the two animals eventually becomes too much for the scientists, Tinker hits upon the idea of taking the Five to stay in the lighthouse he owns at Demon's Rocks, given to him by his father after he had finished using it for an experiment.

The Five next meet Tinker when they go to stay with him at his home,

Big Hollow House, which is a bus ride away from Kirrin. On this second visit he is not *quite* so obsessed with cars!

Tucky (7): The old porter and former railway guard who has worked on the moorland railway since he was a boy. He tells the children all about the network of tunnels running under the moors and gives them an old large-scale map of the railways.

Wilfrid (20): A selfish, mannerless boy of about ten, who has bright blue eyes and yellow hair and is staying with his grandmother, Mrs Layman, at her cottage for a few weeks. When the Five arrive to keep him company he is rude and off-hand with them, telling them to "clear off!" Wilfrid has a great way with animals and when he plays his little wooden flute, even the most timid of wild creatures come to him. Rabbits nestle in his arms and magpies sit on his head. George is very annoyed when even Timmy goes to him. Under the good influence of Julian, Anne, Dick and George, Wilfrid's character does begin to change, and towards the end of his adventure with them he redeems himself by rowing a boat across to Whispering Island where the Five are marooned.

Berta Wright (14): "A slim, pretty little girl with large blue eyes and wavy golden hair", Berta is the daughter of Elbur Wright, an American scientist working with Uncle Quentin on an amazing new invention. Berta has no mother but her father, whom she calls 'Pops', dotes on her, and when she is threatened with kidnap, he leaves her with Uncle Quentin and Aunt Fanny in the hope of putting the kidnappers off the scent. With a few snips of the scissors and a change of clothing Berta is soon transformed into 'Lesley', a boy, with the aim of confusing the kidnappers, who are looking for a long-haired girl. Later Berta is transformed back into a girl and goes to stay with Jo.

Yan (12): A spiky-haired, bare-footed young character with black eyes and very sunburnt skin. He is invariably dirty and poorly dressed in a ragged

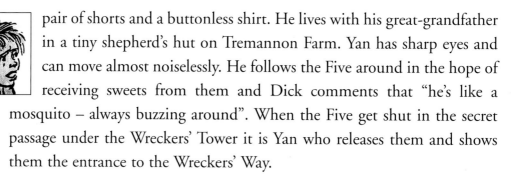

pair of shorts and a buttonless shirt. He lives with his great-grandfather in a tiny shepherd's hut on Tremannon Farm. Yan has sharp eyes and can move almost noiselessly. He follows the Five around in the hope of receiving sweets from them and Dick comments that "he's like a mosquito – always buzzing around". When the Five get shut in the secret passage under the Wreckers' Tower it is Yan who releases them and shows them the entrance to the Wreckers' Way.

THE BADDIES!

In this section meet the vile villains, dastardly deed-doers and not very nice people encountered by the Five!

 Lewis Allburg (5): Known to his friends as Lou, Lewis Allburg works in Mr Gorgio's circus. He is a fine acrobat who can "climb anything anywhere." He is long-limbed with an ugly face and a crop of black curly hair. Like so many of the villains encountered by the Five, Lou has a revolver with which he threatens to kill Timmy. Lou and his partner in crime, **Tiger Dan**, rob rich houses and hide their loot in the **Merran Hills**.

 Mr Andrews (7): A short, dark, little man with a weak face and a nose that is much too big, whom Anne thinks looks rather stupid. Jock tells the Five that Mr Andrews, his step-father, likes to buy cheap and sell expensive. The children wonder why he employs so many men and has so many lorries for such a small farm. Their questions are answered when they discover that he and many of the men working for him are involved in handling stolen property. Mr Andrews is not the brains behind the operation but does seem to organise the men involved in it.

Mr Barling (4): A smuggler who lives on **Castaway Hill** and is determined that the marshes will not be drained. The Five don't know much about Mr Barling, but after he kidnaps George's father and Pierre Lenoir they realise that he is half-mad. He knows the hidden paths across the marshes around Castaway Hill and uses them to bring smuggled goods into the country from small ships anchored out at sea. The local police believe that he is involved in smuggling but he is a clever man and manages to escape detection. After his encounter with the Five he becomes lost in the honeycomb of passages that run through Castaway Hill and Timmy has to help the police rescue him and some of his men.

 **Block (4):** We never learn what Block's first name is, but we do know that he is a sly, unpleasant character. He works as a servant for Mr Lenoir at Smuggler's Top but is actually there as a spy for Mr Barling, the smuggler. Block has an impassive face, like a wax-work, and cold, clever, narrow eyes. He pretends to be deaf and so overhears all sorts of private information which he reports back to his boss. He always wears the same white linen coat and black trousers. He is as strong as a horse and once he realises that the children suspect him of villainy he takes every opportunity he can to be unpleasant to them.

 Mr Curton (6): Staying at the cottage next to the coastguard and pretending to be a journalist, Mr Curton is really the organiser of a group trying to steal Quentin Kirrin's new fuel formula. He is tall and well-built with shaggy eyebrows and a determined mouth. On the surface he pretends to be happy and affable and chats to the Five in a very friendly fashion while trying to pump them for information, but he has a bad temper and is particularly nasty to Martin, Mr Curton comes to a sticky end when he falls down the side of the old quarry and breaks his leg. We last see him being taken off to the prison hospital.

 'Tiger' Dan (5): Dan is the chief clown at Mr Gorgio's circus but the Five have never met anyone less like a clown than the bad-tempered, bullying Dan. When they first meet him he is dirty, shabbily-dressed and chewing on an old pipe. He angrily orders them to move their caravans away from the circus camp, but is even more furious later when he discovers that the Five are camping in the hills above Merran Lake. Dan is a cruel, brutal man with no sympathy for any animal or person who gets in his way. He knocks out **Pongo**, the circus chimpanzee, with a stone, and threatens to poison Timmy. He makes out that he is Nobby's uncle but, in actual fact, is not related to the boy. Tiger Dan and his friend **Lou** use their circus work as a cover for stealing priceless valuables. Their plan is to eventually take their plunder to Holland, where Dan once worked, and sell it.

Dirty Dick (10): An unpleasant character who lives with his mother in a tumbledown cottage on the moors. He has broad shoulders, a shock of untidy hair and a dreadful temper. With the aid of **Maggie Martin**, he hopes to find the jewels stolen from the Queen of Fallonia and hidden near **Two Trees.** However, he is beaten to this prize by the Five, who see that the jewels are taken to the police for safe return to their owner. Dirty Dick comes to a really sticky end when he is stuck in a marsh with a broken ankle.

Mr Gringo (14): Owner of Gringo's Great Fair and prepared to do anything if a wad of money is offered to him. According to Spiky, the roundabout boy, Gringo pays his workers well but drives them like slaves. He is fond of his own comforts and has a double caravan where he lives with his old mother. He also owns a large silver-grey and blue American car. Gringo is responsible for kidnapping George (thinking she is Berta Wright) and keeping her in a house in Twining Village.

 **The Guv'nor (12):** Leader of the Barnies. The Guv'nor is a small man who rarely smiles and is obsessed with looking after the head of **Clopper**, the pantomime horse. He uses the contacts he makes while travelling around Cornwall to organise drug smuggling.

 Junior Henning (18): The spoilt and selfish American boy staying with his father at Finniston Farm. Junior is about eleven years old, never lifts a finger to help if he can avoid it and never bothers to say 'please' or 'thank you'. He leaves his room in a mess and expects breakfast in bed. He finds out the Five's plans by eavesdropping.

 **Mr Henning (18):** Father of Junior and a man intent on buying up every antique he can find at knock-down prices. He even contemplates making an offer for the chapel at Finniston Farm and taking it back to the USA stone by stone! Like his son, Mr Henning has a cunning

streak and when he learns that treasure may be buried under Finniston Farm he tries to get the owner of the farm to sign a contract that will result in the American getting any finds at a bargain price.

 Will Janes (16): A burly man with a thick neck. He once worked on Billycock Farm before going to live with his old mother in a tumbledown cottage on the butterfly farm where she is housekeeper to Mr Gringle and Mr Brent. Will has fallen in with bad company and gives shelter to a group of men who plan to steal two top-secret fighter planes from the Air Force base close to Billycock Hill. He has a violent and dangerous temper and is a bully.

 Johnson (6): Another villain with a revolver! Johnson, a former colleague of Quentin Kirrin, is one of three villains who try to steal his new fuel invention. Johnson and his partner, Peters, parachute down on to Kirrin Island, taking Quentin prisoner and shutting Timmy, there as a guard dog, into a small underground cave. They not only try to steal the formula but also threaten to blow up the entire island!

 Ebenezer and Jacob Loomer (19): Descended from wreckers who used to lure ships on to Demon's Rocks so they could steal their valuable cargoes, Ebenezer and Jacob now try to earn their living showing visitors around the Wreckers' Cave. For years they have searched unsuccessfully for the treasure of gold, silver and pearls believed to have been hidden there by their ancestor, One-Ear Bill. When the Five and Tinker leave the key in the lock of **Demon's Rocks Lighthouse**, Jacob not only goes in and steals valuables but also removes the key and later uses it to trap the children in the lighthouse.

 Maggie Martin (10): A tall woman with a sharp and determined voice. The Five think she looks as hard as nails when they encountered her and Dirty Dick at Two Trees while on the trail of stolen jewels.

Maggie has more brains than her companion but the pair are no match for the Five when it comes to working out the location of the stolen jewels.

 Mr Perton and his gang (8): Owner of **Owl's Dene** and leader of a desperate group of men who, amongst other things, hide escaped convicts from the police. His gang includes Hunchy, Ben and Fred. No guns are actually displayed but Mr Perton does threaten to shoot Timmy.

Peters (6): See **Johnson**.

 Jeffrey Pottersham (11): A scientist who not only wants to sell information to a foreign power but also kidnaps Derek Terry-Kane with the intention of making him divulge his secrets. Pottersham is fascinated by old ruins (he has written a book on the subject) and his knowledge of the secret passages hidden inside the walls of Faynights Castle allows him to find the perfect hiding place for his victim while he waits to take him across the Channel to Europe. Pottersham threatens Timmy with a gun.

 Rooky (8): Ex-bodyguard to Thurlow Kent and a bad-tempered bully. Rooky has a violent temper and scares everyone at Owl's Dene where he is involved in a number of illegal plots. He threatens the Five when they arrive at Owl's Dene looking for Richard Kent, and tries to have Timmy poisoned after the dog bites him.

 Mr Roland and friends (2): A clever villain is a dangerous villain, and Mr Roland - who comes to Kirrin Cottage as a tutor for Julian, Dick and George (Anne had a good report, so didn't need tutoring!) - is a very clever man. Not only does he have an excellent knowledge of all the subjects on the children's school curriculum but he also has a good understanding of Quentin Kirrin's secret work.

He is short, burly and bearded with thin, cruel lips and piercing eyes that never seem to miss a thing. When Anne goes red at the mention of some missing papers, it is Mr Roland who spots it and demands that she tells him what she knows of the matter. He is an agile man – useful for a spy whose job it is to steal secrets - and easily climbs a tree to gather mistletoe for the Christmas decorations at Kirrin Cottage. He has a dry manner of speaking and, while he pretends to be very friendly towards Julian, Dick and Anne, he goes out of his way to upset George. However, this is just a clever way of getting George into trouble and Timothy out of the house. Mr Roland claims that since being bitten by a dog as a boy he dislikes them, but his real fear is that Timothy, whose ears are even sharper than Mr Roland's eyes, will hear him searching Quentin's laboratory for the secret formula he intends to steal. After being discovered once in Uncle Quentin's study he uses his power as tutor to persuade Uncle Quentin that Timothy should be kept outside.

Once he has stolen the formula he passes it to his two friends, Mr Thomas and Mr Wilton, who are staying at Kirrin Farmhouse posing as artists. Fortunately they are all snowed-in, giving the Five a chance to recover the stolen papers.

Sniffer's father (13): We never learn the name of Sniffer's father but we do know that he is not a pleasant man. He treats Sniffer badly and ill-treats his horse, **Clip**. He appears to be the leader of a gang receiving forged hundred-dollar notes, which are flown over from France and dropped by plane on to a lonely stretch of Mystery Moor. He, or one of his gang, knock out Timmy, capture Anne and George and tie them up in a cave in the centre of a hill.

The Stick family (3): About the only good things that can be said about Clara Stick are that she is fond of her dog, **Tinker**, and is a very good cook. She comes to Kirrin Cottage to take the place of Joanna, who has to leave in a hurry to look after her sick mother. Mrs Stick is a sour-faced woman who is quick to grumble and easily upset. When made angry by the Five she refuses to make cakes for tea, and when Uncle Quentin leaves to take Aunt Fanny to hospital, Mrs Stick tries to keep the children very short of food. She is afraid of Timmy and attempts to poison him. When she and her husband kidnap Jennifer Armstrong she shows no remorse that they have shut the small, frightened girl up in a dark and terrifying place.

Her son, Edgar, is a youth of thirteen or fourteen. He is an unpleasant tell-tale, always on the lookout to play sly tricks on the Five but quick to tell his mother if they try to retaliate. He annoys George by singing silly songs about her but runs away when Julian makes a step towards him. Edgar has a wide, red, pimply face with screwed-up eyes and a long nose. Julian and the others call him Spotty Face. He gets little attention from his parents and is probably an unhappy child.

Mr Stick is a seaman on leave from his ship. He is dirty and unkempt but displays good skills of seamanship as he manoeuvres a boat through the dangerous rocks that surround Kirrin Island. He has come to Kirrin to take part in the kidnap plot for which he is to be well paid. He carries a gun and seems quite prepared to use it.

The fourth member of the Stick family is Sarah, a maid working at the Armstrong house who helps to arrange for Jennifer Armstrong to be kidnapped.

Taggart (10): See **Dirty Dick**.

Llewellyn Thomas (17): The wayward son of Bronwen Thomas, who has faked his own murder and imprisoned his mother in the tower room of **Old Towers**. This leaves him free to mine and sell the valuable metal that is buried under Old Towers Hill.

Red Tower and his gang (9): Red Tower lives in a castle-like building at Port Limmersley and is responsible for organising the kidnapping of George and Timmy. He hopes to exchange George for the notebooks containing Uncle Quentin's latest research work. He is a giant of a man with flaming red hair, eyebrows and beard. Julian only has to take one look at his eyes to realise that Red is probably insane. He has mad tempers and takes cruel revenge on anyone who crosses him. He threatens his own men with a gun and tells them: "my orders are always obeyed!" His chief henchman is Markhoff, a short and burly fellow who carries a gun and is only just prevented from shooting Timmy. Other men working for Red are Simmy (the father of Ragamuffin Jo), Jake, Carl and Tom.

 Mr Wooh (21): Mr Wooh is the mathematical wizard at **Tapper's Circus** who can instantly give an answer to the most complex multiplication sum. He is "tall, commanding and handsome" with gleaming eyes, half-hidden by great eyebrows, and a thin, pointed beard. Mr Wooh is the owner of **Charlie the chimp**, who he trains to climb the wall of Professor Hayling's tower and steal secret papers.

THE FAMOUS FIVE AND ANIMALS

We all know that Timmy is the most important animal in the Famous Five adventures but Enid Blyton created many other interesting animals for the stories too. Though she didn't actually own her first pet until she was married, Enid did spend holidays riding, walking dogs and holidaying on farms, as well as drawing wild animals and birds, so she knew lots about all sorts of creatures! She eventually owned a jackdaw, a magpie, four pigeons, two tortoises, several Siamese cats and a couple of terriers! Here are some of the animals we meet in the Famous Five stories:

Enid's parents never allowed their children to keep pets — which may account for Enid's obvious fascination with and love for animals, and her hatred of cruelty towards them. She once nearly broke down a door trying to get to her brother, Hanly, to stop him taking pot shots at innocent birds with his air rifle!

Barker and Growler (5): Nobby's two trained dogs. They are clever, well-behaved terriers who can perform a number of tricks. They can dribble a football around with their noses and walk on their hind legs. Barker nearly dies after eating poisoned meat left out for Timmy by Tiger Dan.

Beauty (11): One of the two pythons owned by Mr Slither, who is camping with the other fair folk at Faynights Field. Beauty likes being handled and enjoys being polished by his master to get rid of mites that lodge themselves under his scales. Beauty likes nothing better than to curl round a friend, though, as Mr Slither points out, it is important not to let him get too good a grip with the end of his tail otherwise the result could be fatal! Jo is very fond of Beauty and takes him with her when she tries to rescue the Five from Faynights Castle. Beauty plays an important part at the end of the adventure when he scares Jeffrey Pottersham and his friends and forces them to retreat into a room where Jo bolts them in.

 Biddy (7): The four-year-old collie belonging to Jock. Biddy lives on **Olly's Farm** and has four puppies.

 Binky (16): The collie dog owned by Toby Thomas of **Billycock Farm** who enjoys shaking paws with everyone he meets – including Timmy. Binky has "bright brown eyes".

 Charlie the chimp (21): The chimpanzee owned by Mr Wooh, who travels with Tapper's Circus, where his skill at playing cricket amazes audiences. Like **Pongo**, the chimp encountered by the Five in *Five Go Off In A Caravan,* Charlie enjoys human company and is ready and willing to help with chores. He is "as strong as ten men" and happily carries the children's tents when they are camping close to the circus camp. The chimp is very fond of **Mischief**, Tinker's little pet monkey. Charlie loves sweets and bananas and opens the bolt on his cage door himself when he wants to go for a walk!

Chippy (Short stories): A tiny brown monkey with a comical face owned by Bobby Loman. The Five first see Chippy up a tree clutching a stolen barley sugar.

Chummy (Short stories): A large cross-bred Alsatian dog also owned by Bobby Loman. After his grandfather threatens to have the dog put to sleep for biting someone, Bobby, Chummy and Chippy, his pet monkey, run away to Kirrin Island where the Five discover them in hiding.

 Clip (13): A small skewbald horse owned by Sniffer's father. The pony is overworked and under-fed. When he goes lame he is brought to Captain Johnson's riding school for treatment. After a rest in the stable

Clip is able to resume work pulling Sniffer's caravan.

Clopper (12): Not a real animal at all but a canvas pantomime horse operated by two men. Clopper is the most popular act at The Barnies' travelling shows. His head is beautifully modelled with eyes that can open, close and swivel. His mouth too can be opened and closed to reveal large teeth. His skilled operators can make him march, tap-dance, jump like a kangaroo and sit down cross-legged. Inside his head is a secret compartment where the Guv'nor conceals smuggled drugs.

Curly (16): The piglet owned by Benny Thomas at Billycock Farm, and so named because of his curly tail. Curly takes an active part in the rescue of Jeff Thomas and Ray Wells after falling into the cave in which the pair are being held prisoner. Curly carries a message back to Billycock Farm written in charcoal on his back!

Dai, Bob, Tang, Doon, Joll, Rafe and Hal (17): The seven dogs belonging to Morgan Jones of **Magga Glen Farm**. Although these dogs do not endear themselves to George after three of them attack Timmy, they more than make up for this when they help Morgan save Aily, her father and the Five after they are captured by Llewelyn Thomas and his miners while exploring the underground passages and river that runs through **Old Towers Hill.**

Dobby (5): The horse owned by Julian's family that was once used to pull the pony cart. When not being borrowed by friends, Dobby spends most of his time in a field close to the children's home. In *Five Go Off In A Caravan* he pulls one of the two small caravans used by the Five.

Fany (17): The little lamb belonging to Aily. It is because Fany frisks off down the tunnel next to the underground river under Old Towers Hill that the Five and Fany are caught by the miners working there.

Growler (5): See **Barker and Growler**.

Jet (15): The lively little black-and-white mongrel is owned by Guy Lawdler, and his name is short for 'Jet Propelled'. He has a "ridiculously long tail" which is always wagging. Blind in one eye, his other eye is exceedingly bright. As with the other small dogs the Five meet, Timmy gets on well with Jet.

Liz (13): One of the strangest-looking dogs that the Five ever meet is Liz, the ex-circus dog owned by Sniffer. Liz is part spaniel, part poodle with odd bits of something else. When the children see her they think she looks like a hearthrug, and Timmy can't make her out at all, particularly when she walks up to him on her back legs and starts to perform forward rolls in front of him. The two dogs soon become good friends, however.

Mischief (19/21): The small, brown-eyed monkey owned by Tinker Hayling. Despite being full of mischief, it is almost impossible to dislike the little creature. Joanna, the cook, is particularly fond of the monkey and gives him titbits. At first Timmy is wary of him – particularly after he takes his bone - but when Mischief offers Timmy a biscuit as a peace offering the two become firm friends, with Mischief curling up between Timmy's front legs to sleep. Mischief finds a gold coin that helps the Five to discover the whereabouts of the wreckers' hoard of treasure at Demon's Rocks. When Tapper's Circus comes to Big Hollow House, Mischief becomes good friends with Charlie the chimp.

Nosey (18): The tame jackdaw at Finniston Farm owned by Henry and Harriet Philpot. The bird has been a pet of the twins since they nursed it back to health after it fell down a chimney, breaking its wing. Like most jackdaws, Nosey is attracted to bright objects and early on in the story tries to steal Dick's watch. Later Nosey, together with **Snippet**

the dog, discovers the passage that runs between the site of Finniston Castle and the old chapel.

Old Lady (5): The elephant at Mr Gorgio's Circus who likes bathing in the lake and squirting water over anyone who comes near.

Pongo (5): The mischievous chimpanzee at Mr Gorgio's circus amuses the children with his antics but is extremely strong and can be fierce if he sees anyone he cares for being hurt. Pongo is a great mimic and will copy the actions of those around him. He gets on well with Timmy but will insist on trying to shake hands with the dog's tail instead of his paw! A bit of a pickpocket, he is particularly fond of anything that he can eat, though he is rather surprised when a sweet sticks his teeth together. He enjoys ginger-beer almost as much as the children and is given his own bottle when they have a picnic. If told off for naughty behaviour he covers his face with his paw but peeps through his fingers. He is a great help in protecting the children from Tiger Dan and Lou in *Five Go Off In A Caravan*. He is knocked out by a large stone thrown at him by Tiger Dan but by the end of the adventure has managed to get his revenge.

Despite the popular saying: 'lashings of ginger beer', this phrase never actually appears in the Famous Five books - though there are lashings of hard-boiled eggs, peas and potatoes in *Five Go Down To The Sea*, and 'lashings of treacle' in *Five Have A Mystery To Solve!*

Sally (14): The tiny black poodle owned by Berta Wright has a sharp little nose, quick eyes and slim legs. Her woolly fur is cut into a "fashionable look". Despite being much smaller than Timmy, Sally has sharp teeth and Berta tells the children that, if provoked, Sally can make a good impression on somebody's leg with them! As with most other dogs they meet, Timmy gets on well with Sally.

Snippet (18): The tiny black poodle owned by Henry and Harriet Philpot of Finniston Farm. Snippet, together with Nosey the jackdaw, discovers a way into the tunnel that runs from the site of Finniston Castle to the old chapel.

 Tinker (3): The dog belonging to the Stick family has a dirty white coat and is rather mangy and moth-eaten to look at. He is re-named 'Stinker' by the Five. He usually has his tail down between his legs and is terrified of Timmy, who chases him as if he were a rabbit!

 Trotter (5): The milkman's sturdy black horse borrowed by the Five to pull the girls' caravan in *Five Go Off In A Caravan*. He gets on with Dobby and is very fond of Timmy. His comical antics amuse the children, particularly when he tries to snuggle under one of the caravans with Timmy!

OUT AND ABOUT WITH THE FAMOUS FIVE

Enid Blyton loved the English countryside, and often wrote poems about it. She had spent several holidays on the Suffolk coast with friends in her youth and, when her own children arrived, took a holiday house on the Isle of Wight. Later, Enid and her family spent holidays in Dorset, where they explored caves and castles, took long walks and hired boats. This love of the outdoors cannot have failed to have transferred itself on to the pages of the books she wrote. Here are just a few of the places and activities the Five enjoyed.

In *The Story Of My Life*, Enid Blyton wrote: 'Such things as going off to the seaside, or staying on farms were just as much a delight to me as they are to you. Every shining, glittering moment was packed away complete into my memory, to be brought out and used again in books about the seaside or country.'

Camping

Camping at High Moors (7): The Five's first camping trip is to High Moors, accompanied by Mr Luffy. High Moors is a vast and lonely stretch of moorland with poor soil and only a handful of scattered farms. Heather grows in abundance on the moor and the Five often hear the cry of the curlew. Close to where the Five are camping are a number of valleys: Roker's Vale, Kilty Vale and Crowley Vale. The latter is renowned for having some of the rarest insects in Britain. The small towns nestling in these valleys are joined by a network of railways. In places, the track runs through long tunnels bored under the moors. Dotted over the moors are vent holes where the smoke from the old-time steam engines that hauled the carriages can escape. These vent holes are covered with iron bars to prevent people crossing the moors from falling down them. The Five know nothing of these

railways when they first arrive on the moors and Anne is terrified when she hears a rumbling noise and then sees masses of steam shooting out of the ground. She believes that she has been sitting close to a volcano and rushes down to find Mr Luffy to warn him! He explains about the trains and the vent holes and 'Anne's volcano' becomes a private joke between them. Close to where the Five are camping is Olly's Yard, a disused railway yard close to where a disused tunnel has been bricked up. The yard is looked after by 'Wooden Leg' Sam who warns the Five of mysterious spook trains that run at night.

A cycling tour (8): The very first cycling tour that the Five go on takes place during the Easter holidays. They have been given two small tents for Christmas and, as the weather is fine and their bikes are in tip-top condition, Aunt Fanny and Uncle Quentin give them permission to go for a cycling holiday. They fill their kit-bags with everything they will need: compass, map, sleeping bags and food, and set off. They plan to cycle forty or fifty miles on their first day. They spend the first night camping close to the Green Pool and plan to spend the second in a flower-lined dell in Middlecombe Woods. But their adventure begins and they are soon off in search of **Owl's Dene.**

Enid Blyton spent several holidays in Suffolk and, like the Five, enjoyed taking long cycle rides to the seaside - often spending the whole day outdoors, accompanied by her friends, Ida and Marjory Hunt, and a large picnic!

A hiking holiday (10): We are not told exactly where the moors are on which the Five go hiking, but the fact that it has a prison on it makes it sound very much like Dartmoor. The moor lies between the boys' and girls' schools. Julian and Dick travel to their meeting place by bus, while the two girls and Timmy travel by train. On the moor they see wild ponies and deer. One night they hear bells ringing and later find out that this is a signal to let the inhabitants know that a prisoner has escaped. The Five pass through a number of villages, including Beacons Village, Reebles and Gathercombe. They intend to spend the four nights of their hike staying at farm houses and it is only when Dick and Anne get lost while looking for Blue Pond Farm that the hiking adventure really begins. They end up at Two Trees, close to the centre of the moor, where they discover thousands of pounds worth of stolen jewels.

Camping on Kirrin Common (15): After getting annoyed at people laughing at Timmy when he has to wear a cardboard collar to stop him scratching stitches in his ear, George goes off camping on Kirrin Common with him. She is later joined by Anne and finally by the two boys. They camp close to a ruined cottage and use a spring for water and a nearby pool for bathing. Needless to say, the old cottage soon becomes the centre of a new adventure!

Camping on Billycock Hill (16): Shaped like an old billycock hat, Billycock Hill is partly heather-clad and partly sloping meadowland where cows and sheep graze. Nestling at the foot of the hill is **Billycock Farm** where Toby Thomas, a school friend of Julian's and Dick's, lives with his

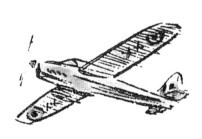

parents and younger brother. For their camp-site the Five choose a spot halfway up the hill, close to a spring and next to a giant gorse bush, which will give them shelter and also a fine view. George reckons that it is "the best camp we've ever had". From here they can also see the airfield where new fighter planes are tested. Billycock Hill is noted for its butterflies, including many rare species, and situated close to where the Five decide to camp is a butterfly farm. Though rather run-down, the great glass-houses where the butterflies are bred are well-maintained. The Five are also close to the Billycock Caves.

The Chalet (17): The large wooden hut halfway up the mountain on

Magga Glen Farm where the Five stay while in Wales. The Chalet is fully equipped with bunk beds, a cooking stove and cupboards full to bursting with tinned food, rugs and crockery, and has a wonderful view across the valley to **Old Towers Hill**.

Camping in Cromwell's Corner Field (21): The Five go to stay with Tinker Hayling at **Big Hollow House** and decide to camp in the field at the end of the garden where Tapper's Circus has set up camp. This is the easiest camping the Five have done as Jenny, the housemaid, prepares most of their food for them.

Caravanning

Caravanning in Merran Hills (5): After watching a circus parade the children decide to go caravanning. They borrow two caravans and use Dobby, their pony, to pull one and the milkman's pony, Trotter, to pull the other. The five set up camp in a hollow in the Merran Hills which shelters them from the wind. It is a peaceful place with birch trees close by, heather in abundance and harebells growing in rock crevices. There is a rocky ledge where they can sit and eat their picnics overlooking Merran Lake. Anne calls the place "Lake View". The lake is a splendid place for swimming with its sandy bottom and crystal clear water. They drink water from one of the many springs that gurgle from the hillside. A fast flowing stream gushes out of the hillside close by. The Five buy all the food they need from Farmer Mackie's wife. They also meet Nobby, the circus boy, and have an exciting adventure.

Ravens Wood (9): George and Timmy are kidnapped by Jo's father, Simmy, and taken to this wood in his caravan. The rest of the Five take the bus there to track them down but the wood is so large and dense that they get lost and are forced to spend the night, huddled under a bush, until they are rescued by Jo.

Caravanning at Faynights Castle (11): On their second caravan holiday the Five borrow old-fashioned, gypsy-style caravans that are parked in a field close to **Faynights Castle**. The boys' caravan is painted red with decorations in black and yellow, while the girls is blue with a blue and yellow pattern. Each caravan has high wheels, a door at the front with steps up to it and a jutting roof with carving around the edge. The caravans have been modernised inside with folding-down bunk-beds, little sinks, small larders and a set of shelves. Cork carpets help to keep out the draughts.

Castles

Faynights Castle (11) The castle is several miles from the coast and set on top of a high hill. It originally had four towers but only one of these now remains complete, while the other three are ruined. The main gateway is no longer used and has been filled in with a wrought iron screen. Visitors who pay to look round the ruin enter through a turnstile set at the base of a small tower. A high wall runs round the castle, though parts of this have fallen down and lie half buried in grass and weeds at the bottom of the hill. The castle walls are over two metres thick and contain a secret passage. The view from the castle is magnificent and sentries would have been  able to see for miles around the surrounding countryside. There is a small village close to the castle and a number of caravans park in the nearby Faynights Field. (See Chapter 4, *Where was Kirrin Castle?*)

Finniston Castle (18): A small castle built in Norman times but burnt down by enemies in 1192. Over the years all the stones were removed from the site and people forgot the castle's exact location. But, while digging in a rabbit hole on **Finniston Farm**, Timmy and Snippet uncover the castle's midden (rubbish dump) and this gives the Five a clue to the whereabouts of the secret passage that was once supposed to run from the castle to the chapel.

Caves

The cave on Kirrin Island (3): Until *Five Run Away Together*, George believed that no caves existed on Kirrin Island. It is Dick who first spots the cave as the Five return to the island after exploring the old wreck. The cave entrance is almost completely hidden by rocks and is only visible from one point on the shore. It has a floor of fine white sand and is perfectly dry. Round one side runs a rocky ledge on which the Five can store tins of food and spare torch batteries. A really useful feature of the cave is that it has a roof-top entrance leading up on to the cliff. This is partly hidden from above by bramble bushes. Julian ties a knotted rope round the roots of a large bush growing close by and the children use this to climb in and out of the cave. As the cave floor is so sandy and soft Timmy can simply jump down on to it.

The cave on Mystery Moor (13): On **Mystery Moor**, close to the deserted sand quarry, is a strange-shaped hill honeycombed with passages and with a cave at the centre. Here Sniffer's father holds George and Anne captive in an attempt to find out what the two boys have done with packets of forged hundred-dollar bills that were dropped on to the moor by a low-flying aircraft.

Billycock Caves (16): A network of caves close to **Billycock Hill** which are open to the public. The entrance is properly paved and there is a large white notice-board instructing visitors to keep to the rope-marked ways. Once through the two metre high entrance there is a series of small caves, which lead into a large, magnificent cave full of what look like gleaming icicles. These are stalagmites growing up from the cave floor and stalactites hanging down from the roof of the cave. The splendour of the place reminds Julian of being inside a cathedral. In places the stalagmites shine with all the colours of the rainbow and elsewhere they have formed so close together that they form "a snow-white screen".

There are many forks and unmarked passages in the cave system and it is very easy for visitors who do not follow the marked routes to become lost. Jeff Thomas and Ray Wells are kept prisoner in one of the unexplored caves by foreign agents intent on stealing fighter aircraft from the air base close to Billycock Hill. (See chapter 4: *Where Was Kirrin Castle?*)

Wreckers' Cave at Demon's Rocks (19): The entrance to the Wreckers' Cave is through a large hole at the base of some very high cliffs. Lanterns, set up by Jacob and Ebenezer Loomer who guide visitors round the caves, shed a little light, but inside the cave is damp and cold with many large puddles in the floor. Once inside, a tunnel twists round and leads downwards until you are walking under the sea itself and the noise of the ocean booming can be heard overhead. The tunnel eventually opens out into an extraordinary cave with a very high roof and irregular ridges running round the walls. The wreckers once stored crates and boxes they stole from wrecked ships on these natural shelves. After this cave there is a maze of tunnels, which flood at high tide making them dangerous to explore.

Circuses

Mr Gorgio's Circus (5): The first circus encountered by the Five belongs to Mr Gorgio. They never actually see a performance but, when the circus is camped in a wide circle close to the shore of Merran Lake, Nobby takes them round to meet some of the animals. They are particularly fond of Pongo, the chimpanzee, Barker and Growler, two of the circus dogs, and Old Lady, the elephant. They also meet Larry, the elephant keeper, Rossy who is in charge of the horses, and Lucilla, a wizened little woman in charge of the monkeys, who is also a wonder at curing sick animals. It is Lucilla's care of Barker which saves his life after he is poisoned.

In her autobiography, Enid Blyton wrote: 'I loved the circus so much as a child... I went behind the scenes once and I never forgot it. I was about nine years old then... before long my imagination had created a whole circus - and so, naturally, when I grew up and wanted to write, one of the things I found it easy to do was to write books about circuses.'

Tapper's Circus (21): Owned by 'Old Grandad' Tapper, this circus has an ancient charter allowing it to stay at Cromwell's Corner Field, close to Big Hollow House, once every ten years. Amongst the attractions at the circus are Charlie, the chimp who plays cricket, Dead-Shot Dick, The Boneless Man, Monty and Winks the clowns, and Mr Wooh, who is amazing at instantly solving very difficult mathematical problems.

Farms

Finniston Farm (18): Set in the heart of rural Dorset, Finniston Farm has been owned by the Philpot family for generations. The farmhouse is a large, three-storey building with red and white roses rambling over its whitewashed walls and round its rather small windows. The farmhouse is entered through an ancient oak door that once hung in Finniston Castle. There are many old beams inside, and

in the great barn oak beams soar up into the roof, reminding Julian of a cathedral. Many of the out-buildings are tiled with the massive grey stone tiles that are such a feature of old Dorset buildings. Close by is a grain store which was once the castle chapel. Enid Blyton based Finniston Farm on a real farm she knew. (See Chapter 4: *Where Was Kirrin Castle?*)

Magga Glen Farm (17): The Five are sent to the small village of Magga Glen, high up in the Welsh mountains, one December to recuperate after having bad colds. They stay at Magga Glen Farm, the home of Glenys Jones and her son, Morgan. So that they can be on their own the Five are allowed to stay in the Chalet, a large hut-like building part-way up the mountain-side, which is well-equipped for holidaymakers with crockery, plenty of tinned food, a stove and rows of bunk-beds. Here they take their toboggans and skis and

enjoy winter sports on the hillsides. From the Chalet they can see across to **Old Towers**, a large, lonely house set into Old Towers Hill.

Olly's Farm (7): Bought by Mr Andrews for his wife and her son Jock, this farm is on the high moors in poor farming country. Mr Andrews has spent a lot of money on the farm and it has a new dairy, neat sheds and plenty of new farm machinery, including a binder and two tractors. There is even a grand piano in the drawing room! Mr Andrews employs many men to work on the farm but, with the exception of Will, the others take little interest in their work. In a large locked shed Mr Andrews keeps a number of ex-army lorries. Jock thinks his stepfather bought them because they were cheap but there seems little use for such a large number of lorries on such a small farm.

Tremannon Farm (12): Set in the heart of rural Cornwall this is the home of Mr and Mrs Penruthlan and is where the Five go to spend a quiet summer holiday. It is four miles from the nearest station and is described as "one of the quietest places in the kingdom". The farm has no electricity and the rooms are lit by either oil lamps or candles. The bedrooms given to the children are sparsely furnished, but the views from the windows are spectacular: miles and miles of cornfields, pasture-land, winding lanes and, in the distance, "the dark blue brilliance of the Cornish sea". The farm livestock includes horses, sheep and hens as well as the three collies: Bouncer, Nellie and Willy, and Ben the Scottie dog. Included in the many outbuildings is a very large barn, described as the best in the district, where The Barnies come to perform. Unknown to Mr Penruthlan and his wife, this barn contains the entrance to **The Wreckers' Way**.

Houses

Big Hollow House (21): The home of Tinker and Professor Hayling on the edge of Big Hollow Village, a bus ride away from Kirrin. The house has been owned by the family for hundreds of years, and the Professor has an ancient parchment granting the family the rights to the field next to their garden, known as Cromwell's Corner, for all time. In the garden is a tall, slender tower with a rough stone wall partly covered in creepers, with "curious tentacle-like rods sticking out at the top". This is where the Professor carries out his experiments and also stores many of his top secret papers.

Hill Cottage (20): The hilltop home of Mrs Layman has wonderful views across the nearby harbour and Anne thinks the tiny cottage looks just like something out of a fairy tale. It has a thatched roof, small windows, a crooked chimney and a front door that leads straight into the kitchen. Narrow, crooked stairs lead up to a long, darkish room with black beams. As there is no gas or electricity in the cottage, cooking is done on an oil-stove. The cottage is lit by ancient oil lamps, while a well in the garden provides them with water.

Owl's Dene (8): Named after the screech owls that inhabit its grounds, this old Tudor mansion with tall chimneys is situated on lonely Owl's Hill, where Mr Perton and his gang plan their crimes. The house has large, rambling grounds and a high wall all around it, with great wrought iron gates that open and close automatically. The house is very self-contained with its own cows, hens and ducks, as well as a vegetable patch. There are, however, few comforts at Owl's Dene, with no water, gas or electricity supplies. Julian, George, Anne, Timmy and Richard Kent go to Owl's Dene in search of Dick after he is mistakenly kidnapped. While attempting to free him, they discover a secret room where escaped convicts are hidden.

Two Trees (10): Close to the centre of the moor that lies between the boys' and girls' schools stands Two Trees, a once grand house but now a blackened ruin. The house is reached along a very narrow track. It is so narrow that fire engines were unable to reach the house in time to extinguish the flames that so damaged it all those years ago. The two huge trees which give the

house its name, and which stand at each end of the house, were also burnt in the fire. The Five camp in the underground room next to the cellars at Two Trees, where the servants once had their quarters. While they are there, the Five run into Dirty Dick and Maggie Martin, who are looking for stolen jewels hidden by a criminal named Nailer.

Next to Two Trees is the small lake of Gloomy Water, where a ruined boathouse nestles up a short backwater. When the Five visit the lake in search of the treasure they have heard about, they find that the boathouse still contains three boats and a raft. They use the raft to row out on to Gloomy Water looking for clues to the whereabouts of the treasure and beat the two criminals to it, leaving them stuck in Green Marshes, where they have to be rescued by the police.

Moors

High Moor (7): See **Camping** section.

Mystery Moor (13): The Five visit Mystery Moor while on holiday at Captain Johnson's Riding School and Ben, the local blacksmith, tells the children that the moor got its name after the Bartle Family, who once owned the moor and built the railway, disappeared suddenly and were never seen again. From that day on, Misty Moor became known as Mystery Moor. A large area of open moorland, Mystery Moor stretches for miles from the edge of the village of Milling Green to the coast. It is a wild and desolate area with few farmhouses or cottages, though dotted over the moor are freshwater springs where animals and travellers can quench their thirst. There are great stretches of springy grass and masses of heather, and in the spring it is ablaze with gorse. At other times thick sea mists blow in, making it impossible to see your hand in front of your face. At its eastern edge, where it meets the sea, the

cliffs are unclimbable and reefs of rock stretch out into the ocean. Towards the sea the ground becomes sandy and there is a large quarry, and a smaller pit, which once supplied sand to the surrounding district. These are now disused and deserted but the remains of a railway track, once used to transport the sand from the quarry to Milling Green, is still visible in places, though the rails are now rotten or missing. The ancient steam engine with its tall chimney, once used to pull the wagons, lies rusted and broken in a large gorse bush. Close to the quarry is a sandy hill, honeycombed with passages, where Anne and George were held captive by Sniffer's father.

Secret places and passages

The Secret Way (2): Running underground between Kirrin Cottage and Kirrin Farmhouse is The Secret Way, a tunnel dug centuries before, when people wanted to hide from their enemies. The Five find an old cloth with directions written in Latin to the entrance of The Secret Way. They solve the Latin riddle and discover the entrance in Uncle Quentin's study. They press a sliding

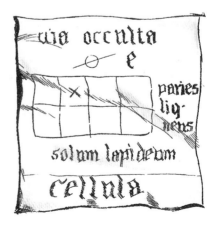

panel and pull a handle and a stone in the floor slides downwards, revealing a dark hole. The Secret Way is narrow, dark, cold and damp and in places the children have to stoop almost double to move along it. At one point the roof has fallen in and they have to squeeze over the sandy soil to continue their journey. About halfway along the passage the tunnel has been enlarged to form a resting place with an old stone bench. Eventually they discover a ladder of iron staples leading upwards through a chimney of rock and stone. At the top an old oak door blocks the way, but a moving panel lets them escape and they are surprised to find themselves inside a cupboard in one of the bedrooms at Kirrin Farmhouse.

Smuggler's Top (4): A good way along the coast from Kirrin is Smuggler's Top, the home of Pierre and Marybelle Lenoir. It is old and mysterious and built on the top of Castaway Hill with one side on the very edge of the steep cliff that falls away to the marshes which surround the hill. On the east side of the house is a round tower that looks out across the marshes to the sea. Smuggler's Top, like many ancient buildings, has secret passages built within its walls which were originally used by smugglers. At least two of these lead to the catacombs that honeycomb Castaway Hill. The entrance to the first one is by the front door and is useful for hiding Timmy from Mr Lenoir. Sooty Lenoir takes the children into an oak-panelled room and presses the corner of one of the panels. A small part of the panel slides open. Inside is a lever which, when pulled, causes a larger panel to open. The children and Timmy squeeze through into a narrow passage which

On a visit to Seckford Hall Farm, Enid had her own holiday adventure. Though now restored, the 15th century mansion was then partly in ruins and the children spent hours playing within it, discovering a 'haunted' bedroom and a *real* secret passage!

eventually leads them to a cupboard in Sooty's bedroom. When he is not out walking with the children or being smuggled into one of their rooms, Timmy has to live in this secret passage where he spends his time chasing rats!

A second passage at Smuggler's Top begins in Marybelle's room. A trap-door under the carpet leads down into a deep pit with passages leading off it. The children use a rope ladder to descend into the pit but poor old Timmy has to be lowered down in a laundry basket.

The third secret passage in the old house has its entrance in a window seat. This, like the passage in Marybelle's room, leads to the network of passages known as **The Catacombs.**

Castaway Marshes (4): There is nothing more mysterious than a marsh, particularly when it is close to the sea and wreathed in mist. The secret paths that cross the marshes near Castaway were once used by smugglers to carry goods from ships anchored out at sea to the mainland. The whereabouts of these paths are now known to very few people. Mr Lenoir, who owns the marshes, wants to drain them so that houses can be built on the land.

The Catacombs (4): When the Five visit 'Sooty' Lenoir at Smuggler's Top, he takes them to explore the passages that riddle Castaway Hill and which are know locally as The Catacombs. Most of the old houses built on the hill have an entrance down to the tunnels. They were originally used by smugglers bringing smuggled goods over the marshes to the mainland.

Tunnels in the Merran Hills (5): In a hollow in the Merran Hills is the entrance to a series of tunnels that were created over many years by fast-flowing underground streams. The Five discover the entrance hidden under the very spot where they have parked one of their caravans. They descend into the tunnels using footholds made from strong nails hammered into the walls, then follow a passage into a cave. They find further passages and a huge cavern with another passage leading off it. Following this, they come to a rocky ledge where thieves have hidden a huge amount of stolen goods: jewels, silver and gold.

Some of the streams responsible for hollowing out the tunnels still run through the hillside and the Five wade up one of them in an attempt to find another way out after they become trapped.

Olly's Yard (7): Olly's Yard, a disused railway yard close to where the Five are staying on the moors, is near to the entrance to one of the moorland railway tunnels, close to where two tunnels meet. One of these tunnels has been bricked up, but a gang of crooks has built a secret door in the wall and is using the tunnel and an old railway engine for the transportation of stolen goods.

The secret room at Owl's Dene (8): The secret room at Owl's Dene is hidden behind a bookcase and is used to hide escaped convicts from the police. Julian discovers it after following the sound of snoring made by Solomon Weston who was hiding there.

The passage under Kirrin Bay (6): One of the most amazing secret passages used by the Five is that which runs under the sea-bed from Kirrin to Kirrin Island. One entrance can be found in the only room in Kirrin Castle which isn't completely ruined. A stone in the fireplace recess can be swung open to reveal steps leading downwards through the castle wall. The passage is very narrow at first but soon broadens out, leading first to an enormous cave and then on to a number of smaller caves (Timmy was shut up in one of these by the villains in *Five On Kirrin Island Again)*. The passage then splits into three, and the left-hand tunnel in turn splits into three. Anyone not knowing their way could easily become lost in this maze of passages. Rock falls part block the way in places, but the passage eventually leads to an entrance in the quarry behind Kirrin Cottage. Timmy successfully finds the route from the island to the quarry and then takes Julian, Dick and Martin Curton back along it. Peters and Johnson, two villains trying to steal one of Uncle Quentin's discoveries, get lost in the passages and Timmy has to be sent in to guide them out!

Secret entrance at Kirrin Castle (1,6): The Five find an old parchment plan of Kirrin Castle in a tin-lined wooden box on the old wreck during their first adventure. The plan is in three parts, one showing the dungeons, one showing the ground floor, and the third part showing the upper rooms of the castle. From it they discover the whereabouts of one of the entrances to the castle dungeons and also learn of the hidden gold ingots. The children traced a copy of the plan just before Uncle Quentin sells it, yet in *Five On Kirrin Island Again* it appears that they still have the original – perhaps Uncle Quentin managed to buy it back. They study it and come to the conclusion that Uncle Quentin must have discovered the second entrance to the dungeons that they failed to find.

The passage in Faynights Castle (11): When Timmy gets tired of waiting outside Faynights Castle for the children to return from their visit he sniffs around looking for another way in - and discovers the entrance to a secret passage that runs through the hollow wall of the castle. Part of the wall has crumbled, leaving a small gap partway up the outer castle wall. The children follow Timmy's route and then squeeze through and find themselves in a low, narrow passage. They follow this and arrive at some steps. These lead down to a wider passage that turns off at right angles and goes under the castle courtyard. A further flight of steps takes them to a small room, and from here it leads to the spiral stairs going up into the remaining tower of the castle.

The Wreckers' Way (12): On the Cornish coast close to Tremannon Farm is an old house with a tower once used by wreckers. On dark and stormy nights the evil wreckers would set a light in the tower-room to lure ships on to the rocks in Tremannon Cove. The house is now deserted and in a state of ruin. The massive old door that led to the tower has fallen and lies like a large slab on the floor. A spiral staircase leads up to the tower room but the walls have started to crumble and the Five have to take great care when going to the top of the tower. Downstairs in the largest of the four rooms is the entrance to a secret passage known as The Wreckers' Way. This runs from the coast to the farm and was used a century or more ago by wreckers carrying goods they had collected from beached ships to an inland hiding place. The location of the way was a closely guarded secret that was handed down to Grandad by his father. He in turn passes the secret on to Yan, who eventually shows the Five the entrance hidden behind a massive boulder. The passage has a number of branches that the Five do not explore but at least one of them reaches to the coast.

The tunnel on Kirrin Common (15): The Five are searching for blueprints stolen by a thief named Paul and hidden on Kirrin Common. The only clue they have is that it is somewhere behind a large stone slab. They discover the slab close by the spring and the old ruined cottage. The Five follow the tunnel revealed behind it down and along until they exit in the middle of a partially excavated Roman camp site.

Under Old Towers Hill (17): Aily, the little Welsh girl who knows the mountains like the back of her hand, shows the Five the entrance to a pot-hole which drops down into a tunnel. This leads downwards, eventually taking them to one of the old cellars at Old Towers.

The passage from Finniston Castle to Finniston Chapel (18): Legend has it that a passage once ran from Finniston Castle to Finniston Chapel. One entrance to this passage is discovered under a wooden trapdoor in the grain store on Finniston Farm (once the castle chapel), while the other is in the castle dungeons. The Five discover the latter when the Harries' pets, Snippet and Nosey, go down a rabbit hole and return with an ancient dagger and an old jewelled ring.

Demon's Rocks Lighthouse (19): The lighthouse was built during the 1890s to prevent ships from being dragged on to the dangerous Demon's Rocks by strong currents. Money for its construction was provided by a rich man whose daughter had been drowned in a ship wrecked on the rocks. When a new, more powerful lighthouse was built at High Cliffs the old building became disused and was bought by Professor Hayling, who later gave it to his son, Tinker. The lighthouse is built well out on the rocks and at high tide can only be reached by boat from the stone jetty on the quay. When the tide is out it is possible to wade across to it. Stone steps lead up from the rocks to the stout door, opened with a very large key, and inside an iron spiral-staircase leads up to the various rooms. First there is the store room and then the oil room where the oil to power the light was once kept. Next is one of the few rooms with a window, used as a bedroom. Further up the staircase is the living room. This has a higher roof than other rooms in the building. In it is a table, a desk and some chairs, as well as a paraffin stove for boiling water and frying food, and an oil lamp to provide light for the room. Over the little sink is a tank with a pipe leading to a 'catch tank' fixed on the outside west wall of the lighthouse to collect rainwater. At the top of the lighthouse is the lamp room where the great old oil lamp once shone out to warn ships. There are windows all round the lamp room and a small door that leads out on to a gallery. Here a large bell once hung that would be rung during foggy weather to warn ships of the rocks. When the lighthouse was constructed, the builders used a natural tunnel running down into the rocks as part of the foundations. They encased the walls in thick concrete and built the lighthouse on top of this. At the base of the lighthouse is a trapdoor with a ladder leading down a shaft into the tunnel. The Five discover that this tunnel leads to the Wreckers' Cave but that it is dangerous to explore as the sea rushes in at high tide.

(N.B: In *Five Are Together Again* we are told that the lighthouse was later damaged in a storm.)

The passage on Whispering Island (20):
Whispering Island is a mysterious place set in the centre of a great harbour. It was once owned by a friend of King James II who had a great castle-like house built in the middle of the woods that cover much of the island. Legend has it that he took all kinds of treasures there, including superbly sculpted statues, a golden bed encrusted with precious stones, a necklace of large rubies, and a sword with a jewelled hilt. In more recent years the

island was owned by a man and his wife who kept it as a nature reserve. They employed armed watchmen to keep away visitors who might disturb the birds and animals. Lucas, who once worked as a watchman on the island, tells the Five that local people have several names for the place. Some call it Whispering Island on account of the noise made as the wind blows through the trees. Others call it Wailing Island because of the wailing noise made by the wind blowing through the caves and holes in the tall cliffs. Many call it Keep-Away Island because people have never been welcome there. One end of the secret passage on Whispering Island is located in The Wailing Cliffs. It is a slit-like opening with a ditch running down the centre and a slippery ledge on either side. The first part is a natural crack in the rock but further along it becomes man-made. The passage eventually ends at a great iron gate made of criss-crossed iron bars, which leads into the dungeon of the old house. A passage from the dungeon leads to a great cellar. High up on the cellar wall is a small door leading into the castle well-shaft. Enid Blyton based Whispering Island on a real island in Dorset (see Chapter 4, *Where was Kirrin Castle?*).

WHAT'S IT ALL ABOUT?

Which book should you read next? Do you want another summer holiday story or a mystery set on Kirrin Island? This section gives a taste of the adventures in each of the books.

FIVE ON A TREASURE ISLAND (1)
The first great adventure!

Five On A Treasure Island

The Five first meet and become friends, visit Kirrin Castle, explore a wrecked sailing ship, find an old map and make a wonderful discovery.

Julian, Dick and Anne are sent to stay with their cousin, Georgina, at the small seaside village of Kirrin. They have never met her, so are looking forward to the visit. They try to make friends with Georgina but find her to be a strange girl who wishes she was a boy and will only answer to the name of George. Her hair is cut short and she never wears dresses or plays with dolls. At first the four children clash, but gradually they begin to understand each other.

When they go down to the beach the next day, George tells them about Kirrin Island, its castle, and the wrecked sailing ship that lies in the shallow water close to the island. Her family own the island and George's mother has promised her that one day soon it will be George's.

George tells her cousins that she must go and fetch Timothy, her best friend. They are astonished when she returns with a big, bouncy mongrel dog that jumps around them, all wagging tail and licking tongue. George explains that she found Timothy as a pup but because he chewed up so many things in the cottage her parents wouldn't let her keep him. She persuaded one of the local fisher-boys to look after him for her but in return she has to give him all of her pocket money to pay for Timothy's food. Julian suggests that as George has no money for ice-creams but *does* have so many things that they would like to share: Timothy, the old wreck, Kirrin Island and Kirrin Castle - she should accept ice-creams from them, in return for a share of her exciting things. This is agreed and her three cousins are excited and pleased when George suggests that after lunch they row out to look at the old wreck.

The four children have an exciting afternoon diving down into the clear waters of Kirrin Bay to look at the wrecked sailing ship shimmering in the waters below them. George tells them the story of the lost Kirrin treasure. The ship, which was owned by her family and captained by her great-great-great-grandfather, was bringing gold ingots to land when it was wrecked in a storm. Although divers have been down and explored the wreck thoroughly the gold bars have never been found.

Two days later the four children and Timothy visit Kirrin Island and begin to explore its ruined castle but while they are enjoying themselves a storm blows up, forcing them to shelter in the castle's only near complete room.

Julian goes to watch the crashing waves and sees that the storm has dragged the wreck up from the sea-bed and left it stranded on some of the rocks that surround the island. They are eager to row out to the wreck to look for clues to the whereabouts of the lost treasure but it's too dangerous and they have to wait.

As dawn breaks the following morning the children set out to explore the wreck. They find an ancient box with the letters H.J.K. on the lid, but no treasure. These initials stand for Henry John Kirrin, George's great-great-great-grandfather. The Five take the box home in the hope that it may contain some clue to the lost treasure.

The Five have great difficulty opening the box and decide to throw it out of one of the upstairs windows at Kirrin Cottage, in the hope that it will burst open as it hits the ground. Their plan succeeds, but the noise causes

Uncle Quentin to rush out of his study and demand to know what they are doing. He takes the box away and refuses to let them see what it contains.

Later, while Uncle Quentin is snoozing, Julian creeps into his study and removes the box. Inside is an old parchment showing a plan of what they believe to be Kirrin Castle. Written within the area of the castle dungeons is the word 'ingots'. Dick explains that metal bars are often called ingots and they all become very excited. They trace a copy of the plan and return the box and its contents to Uncle Quentin's study. They decide to ask Aunt Fanny if they can spend a few days camping on Kirrin Island. Their plan is to use their tracing to find the castle dungeons and search for the gold they believe is hidden there.

The children are dismayed though, when a few days later they learn that Uncle Quentin has sold the old box from the wreck. Shortly afterwards they are utterly shocked when he announces that he is about to sell Kirrin Island to the same buyer. No amount of persuasion from the children will make him change his mind and he tells them that if they want to spend a few days on Kirrin Island they had better do so soon, before the sale is completed.

The Five arrive on Kirrin Island and, using the tracing, begin looking for the dungeon entrance. Timmy discovers the old castle well while chasing a rabbit and eventually Anne finds the stone slab covering the steps leading to the dungeons. They go down and find one of the dungeon doors locked. Using an axe brought from Kirrin Cottage, they try to break open the door, but a large splinter chips off and tears into Dick's cheek. Anne and Dick stay above ground while Julian returns to the dungeon where he and George eventually break open the door and find a pile of gold ingots. While they are looking at their exciting discovery, two men appear in the dungeon and threaten the children with a gun. They force George to write a letter to Anne and Dick telling them to come down into the dungeons. They send the note up with Timmy, stuck into his collar. But George has signed the note 'Georgina', which makes Dick suspicious, and he quickly discovers what has happened. The men search for Dick and Anne but cannot find them. Later they pile heavy rocks over the dungeon entrance and leave the island, taking the children's oars with them. With the aid of a rope, Dick climbs down the well-shaft and into the dungeons, where he unbolts the dungeon door and rescues the others. When the men return to the island, Dick tries to draw them into the dungeon, but has to make a quick escape up the well-shaft to prevent being captured himself. The children find the men's boat and smash its outboard motor. They find their oars and row back to Kirrin, where they tell Uncle Quentin and Aunt Fanny the whole story. The police are informed, the villains are captured, and the treasure is recovered. George's father tells her that she can have anything she wants as a reward and she, of course, asks for Timmy.

FIVE GO ADVENTURING AGAIN (2)
Christmas with the Famous Five

Christmas at Kirrin Cottage, an interesting visit and an exciting discovery. Timothy in trouble, stolen papers and a secret passage.

Five Go Adventuring Again

Christmas holidays at Kirrin Cottage do not look like being the fun the Five had hoped for when they learn that they are to have lessons every morning with a new tutor, Mr Roland. Not only is he strict, but he also dislikes dogs which upsets George.

The Five visit Kirrin Farmhouse and, behind a sliding panel, discover an old piece of cloth with strange markings and Latin words on it. Mrs Sanders, the farmer's wife, allows the children to keep the cloth, and they return home determined to learn its secret.

The two boys ask Mr Roland to help them translate the words on the cloth and they discover that it gives directions to the entrance of The Secret Way, which it says they will find in an east facing room with eight wooden wall panels. The children believe that the entrance must be at Kirrin Farmhouse and decide to search for it as soon as possible after Christmas.

On Christmas night George hears a noise downstairs and takes Timothy to investigate. She finds Mr Roland in her father's study and Timothy holds him down on the floor. Mr Roland explains that he heard a noise and came to investigate, but George doesn't believe him. When Uncle Quentin arrives on the scene he is very angry and tells George that in future Timmy must live outside in a kennel. This upsets George and makes her hate Mr Roland even more.

The next morning Julian, Dick and Anne go to Kirrin Farm to search for The Secret Way. While they are there they meet two artists who are staying at the farmhouse over Christmas. Unable to find any clues to The Secret Way, they return home.

That night George creeps down to let Timmy into the house. She takes him into her father's study, which is still warm from from the extinguished log fire, and rubs the dog's chest with camphor. The next morning Quentin discovers that the three most important pages of his research work have been taken from his study during the night. The bottle of camphor is found and George is sent to her father to explain how it got there. She admits that she was in the study but gives her word that she never touched the papers. Her father believes her, but decides she must be punished for bringing Timothy into the house. While he is discussing her punishment with his wife, George notices that there are eight wooden panels on the study wall.

Outside, thick snow begins to fall. Soon Kirrin Cottage will be snowed up. Uncle Quentin returns to his study and says that for her punishment George will be sent to her room for the rest of the day and she will not be allowed to see Timmy for three days.

Later Julian sneaks up to see George and she tells him of her discovery. She believes that Mr Roland has stolen the missing papers and makes Julian promise to follow the tutor if he leaves the cottage. Later Mr Roland goes out in the snow and Julian follows. The tutor meets the artists who are staying at Kirrin Farmhouse and gives them a bundle of papers.

The Five sneak into Uncle Quentin's study and discover that The Secret Way begins under the study floor. The next morning, while their uncle is busy sweeping snow away from the cottage, they go along The Secret Way, up a ladder of iron staples, and find themselves in a secret compartment behind a large bedroom cupboard at Kirrin Farmhouse. The room is being used by one of the artists staying there, and the children begin searching for the stolen papers. The artists return and the children only just manage to escape into the cupboard. As she squeezes through it, George feels some bulky papers in the pocket of one of the coats hanging there and quickly removes them as she scrambles to go back down the ladder to The Secret Way. But Timmy's barking from the passage below has alerted the artists and they discover the entrance and begin following the Five.

George gives the papers to Dick while she stays behind briefly to order Timmy to keep the two artists at bay. When the Five arrive back at the Kirrin Cottage entrance to The Secret Way, Aunt Fanny and Uncle Quentin are there waiting for them. Uncle Quentin is overjoyed to have his precious papers back and amazed at the children's story. Timmy stays in the study that night and, when the two artists appear, he corners them there. Mr Roland is locked in his bedroom until the police arrive to take all three men away. The Five can enjoy the rest of the Christmas holidays without a tutor!

FIVE RUN AWAY TOGETHER (3)
Back on Kirrin Island

Five Run Away Together

Summer at Kirrin, the awful Stick family and off to Kirrin Island. Who is using the old wreck, who screams in the night and what is going on in the dungeons?

The Five are back at Kirrin Cottage for part of the summer holidays but things are gloomy because Aunt

Fanny is ill, Joanna, the cook, has gone off to look after her mother, and Mrs Stick has been employed to take her place. Mrs Stick is a sour woman who does not like having the Five around, and her son, Edgar, is an unpleasant boy who delights in tormenting George with silly songs. Matters reach a crisis when Aunt Fanny is rushed to hospital and the children are left in the care of Mrs Stick. To make matters worse, her husband, a sailor on leave from his ship, also comes to stay. The Five decide to run away and camp on Kirrin Island until Uncle Quentin returns from staying at the hospital with his wife. To put the Sticks off the scent, and to make them believe that they have all gone to stay at Julian, Dick and Anne's home, they leave a railway timetable open and set off across the moors at the back of the cottage as if they are going to the station. When they are out of sight of Kirrin Cottage they make for the next cove along the coast where Dick is waiting with the boat, which is stocked up with tinned food, rugs and cushions and a large bone for Timothy.

When they reach the island they find that the roof of the one complete room in the castle has fallen in and they have to think of somewhere else to sleep. The old wreck is too musty and damp for them to camp in but they see signs that other people have been looking around it. They believe that smugglers are using the wreck and decide they must investigate. On the way back to the island Dick spots the entrance to a cave, and when they explore further they find it is just right for camping in. It has a sandy floor and a roof entrance from the cliff-top that is hidden by brambles.

That night they hear a noise and discover that the Stick family are on the island. They keep watch and see the Sticks go out to the old wreck. The Five wonder what the Sticks are doing on Kirrin Island, and the mystery deepens when the children see them bringing a trunk from the old wreck to the island. The Five 'capture' the trunk, together with cushions and other items the Sticks have taken from Kirrin Cottage and take everything back to their cave.

Later Edgar Stick accidently falls through the hidden cliff-top entrance to the cave and the Five keep him prisoner. They discover that the Sticks have kidnapped a little girl, named Jennifer Armstrong, and that the trunk is full of her clothes and dolls. When Mr and Mrs Stick leave the island the Five discover Jennifer held prisoner in one of the dungeons. They release her, leave Edgar in her place and row back to Kirrin Village, where they explain everything to the police and Uncle Quentin.

Aunt Fanny is recovering from her illness and is soon to return to Kirrin Cottage. Jennifer Armstrong's parents arrive and thank the Five for rescuing her. They want to take their daughter home but she has taken to a life of adventure and persuades them to let her go camping with the Five on Kirrin Island.

FIVE GO TO SMUGGLER'S TOP (4)
Their first adventure away from home

Easter at Smuggler's Top. Mist shrouded marshes with hidden paths and a hill full of secret tunnels. Who is signalling at night and why is Uncle Quentin kidnapped?

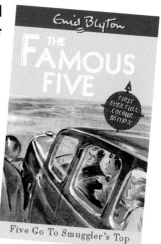

Five Go To Smuggler's Top

After an ash tree falls on Kirrin Cottage and smashes the roof, the Five go to stay with Pierre and Marybelle Lenoir at Smuggler's Top, their lonely house set on top of Castaway Hill and surrounded by marshes. Mr Lenoir doesn't like dogs and they are forced to hide Timmy in one of the many secret passages that are to be found at Smuggler's Top.

Someone is signalling from the tower room and the children try to discover who it is. Their suspicions turn to either Mr Lenoir or his servant, Block. Castaway Hill is honeycombed with tunnels originally used by smugglers and Pierre tells the Five that Mr Barling, who lives close by, is a modern day smuggler.

Quentin Kirrin decides to visit Mr Lenoir to discuss plans for draining the marsh, but on the night of his arrival he and Pierre mysteriously disappear. The children set out to discover what has happened to them.

The boys go to Mr Barling's house but learn from a gardener that he has gone away. Meanwhile George carefully examines the room where her father was sleeping and finds a screw from the window seat on the floor. The children explore and discover a way down to the catacombs through the window seat.

Mr Barling, with the help of Block who is really working for the smuggler, has kidnapped Uncle Quentin to prevent him from draining the marshes. Once drained, Mr Barling would no longer be able to carry out his smuggling operations.

Timmy, who has found his way into the catacombs from the secret passage where he was being hidden, finds Mr Barling, Block and their prisoners and attacks the two smugglers who run off into the tunnels. Timmy then leads Uncle Quentin and Pierre through the catacombs to an entrance at the edge of the marsh. The dog then runs off back into the tunnels.

Meanwhile the children, who are exploring the catacombs, encounter Mr Barling and Block who decide to keep them prisoners in order to persuade Mr Lenoir not to have the marsh drained. Before the smugglers have time to tie up the children Timmy arrives and attacks the smugglers, who run off into the tunnels leaving their lantern behind.

Timmy leads the children to where Uncle Quentin and Pierre are waiting, close to the edge of the marsh, and then guides them through the treacherous marshes back to the road. But as he jumps towards the road Timmy slips and begins sinking into the mud. Luckily a lorry with some planks on board is passing and Uncle Quentin manages to pull the dog to safety. They return to Smuggler's Top and tell their story to Mr Lenoir and the police.

Without a lantern Mr Barling and the other villains have become lost in the maze of underground passages, and the police ask if they can send

Timmy in to find the men. George agrees and Timmy rounds them up like sheep and leads them out to the waiting police.

FIVE GO OFF IN A CARAVAN (5)
Their first holiday on their own

A caravanning holiday in the country. Fun with Nobby and the circus animals but trouble from Tiger Dan and Lou. Why are the two men so keen for the Five to move their caravans and what is the secret hidden inside the Merran Hills?

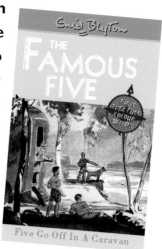

After watching a circus procession, the Five decide to go on a caravanning holiday. They borrow two horse-drawn caravans and set off in the direction taken by the circus. They stop in the Merran Hills, close to where the circus is camped, and make friends with Nobby, an orphan, who is looked after by his uncle, 'Tiger' Dan. Nobby has a wonderful way with animals and introduces them to Pongo, the chimpanzee. Dan and Lou, the circus clown and acrobat, are very unpleasant characters and try to bully the Five into leaving the area. After the children move their caravans further up the hill and park them in a hollow overlooking Merran Lake, Dan and Lou become even more incensed and threaten to poison Timmy.

The Five investigate and discover that they have parked their caravans over the hidden entrance to a secret tunnel used by Lou and Dan to hide stolen goods. After an exciting adventure that takes them into the very heart of the hill, the villains' plans are thwarted and Nobby gets a job looking after the animals on a nearby farm.

FIVE ON KIRRIN ISLAND AGAIN (6)
Back on Kirrin Island again

Five On Kirrin Island Again

Uncle Quentin's secret work on Kirrin Island and a passage that runs underneath the sea-bed itself. Strangers after Quentin's secrets and a race against time to save Kirrin Island from total destruction!

Uncle Quentin 'borrows' Kirrin Island and builds a strange tower to help him with some secret experiments that require him having water all around him. The Five meet Martin Curton and his guardian who are staying in the cottage next to the coastguard. The children believe that Mr Curton is a journalist trying to get information about Kirrin Island and Uncle Quentin's work.

Later, while looking for flint arrow-heads in the old quarry behind Kirrin Cottage, the Five discover the entrance to a secret passage but, before they have time to explore it, mysterious happenings begin to occur on the island. Quentin believes that he is not alone and Timmy stays with him to act as guard dog. Quentin agrees to signal every morning and evening and, to please George, agrees to take Timmy with him to the top of the tower so that she can see her pet through the coastguard's telescope.

When George fails to see Timmy she believes that something is wrong and in the middle of the night rows across to the island to find out what has happened. She finds her father a prisoner in part of the dungeon. Men who parachuted on to the island want his secret formula, but he has hidden the notebook with details of his experiment in one of the caves. He gives the notebook to George and tells her to take it back to Kirrin. She goes looking for Timmy and finds him shut in a small cave. She just manages to free him when the men return and, in desperation, she gives the notebook to Timmy who runs off along a passage carrying the notebook in his mouth.

The villains don't realise that George has managed to set Timmy free, and continue to try and force Quentin to reveal his secrets. They threaten that if he does not give them the information they want, they will destroy his equipment – and the island with it.

Meanwhile, Timmy has found his way back to Kirrin Cottage and jumps on Julian's bed. The children are puzzled by how Timmy managed to arrive back on the mainland and amazed that he has Uncle Quentin's precious notebook. They see that Timmy wants them to follow him and set out just as dawn is breaking. To their surprise, he does not take them to the beach but bounds off to the old quarry and makes for the secret passage entrance. The Five find Martin there with spades and the boy explains that Mr Curton is often mixed up in shady schemes. The children suspect that his step-father is behind the happenings on the island. Martin asks if he can help them and, leaving Anne to explain what has happened and get help taken to Kirrin Island, they set off along the tunnel behind Timmy. Soon after they go, Anne hears a noise and sees Mr Curton entering the quarry, but the man falls and breaks his leg, which quite pleases Anne!

FIVE GO OFF TO CAMP (7)
A camping holiday on the moors

The lonely high moors with their mysterious railway tunnels and talk of spook trains. Why is Mr Andrews so keen for the Five to keep away from Olly's Yard - and how can a railway engine disappear into thin air?

The Five go on a camping holiday to the wild and desolate moors with Mr Luffy, one of the teachers at the boys' school. A railway system with long tunnels running under the moors links the small towns that

101

lie in the moorland valleys. Close to where the Five are camping is a disused railway yard with a strange old watchman who tells them of mysterious spook trains that come out of the tunnels in the dead of the night with no lights and no driver.

The Five make friends with Jock, who lives with his mother and step-father on the nearby Olly's Farm. Jock does not get on very well with his step-father, Mr Andrews. The man bought the farm for his wife but is disinterested in it and has employed men who seem to have no interest in, or knowledge of, farm work. Julian and Dick are also puzzled by the large number of lorries Mr Andrews keeps for such a small farm. The children tell Jock about the spook trains and the boys, determined to discover the truth about them, set out late one night to watch for them. They see a spook train that seems to disappear into thin air.

When George finds out that she was left out of the night's adventure, she goes off in a sulk with Timmy and has her own adventure. She accidentally discovers one of the old vents that lets smoke out of the tunnels. She and Timmy scrape away at the rusted bars and Timmy suddenly falls through. George scrambles down into the tunnel to rescue her pet and discovers the spook train there. She hears voices, and hides in one of the trucks. The train begins to move and she is amazed when she sees a section of the tunnel wall slide back for the train to go through.

Meanwhile, the boys and Anne are once again exploring the tunnel close to Olly's Yard. Anne is not keen on the dark, old tunnel and decides to return over the top path in the sunlight, where she sees Mr Andrews and some of his men going towards the tunnel. Suddenly the boys are surprised by Mr Andrews and his men and are taken into the secret cave with the spook train and tied up.

After Mr Andrews leaves, George comes out of hiding and cuts her friends free. They begin to explore and discover that the network of caves not only contains the spook train but is also filled with stolen goods. They find the mechanism for working the sliding wall and escape into the main air-vent discovered by George, but the bars prevent them getting out and they are caught.

Back at camp, Anne has told Mr Luffy about the strange adventure and he in turn informs the police who, with the aid of Timmy, round up the gang of thieves.

FIVE GET INTO TROUBLE (8)
Their first cycling holiday

Off into the countryside and a meeting with Richard Kent, which leads the Five into a lot of trouble and big adventure at lonely Owl's Dene.

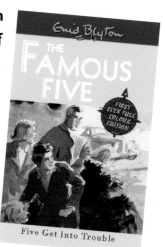

Five Get Into Trouble

The children go on a cycling holiday and meet Richard Kent, a boy of twelve, who tags along with them for part of the way. They plan to camp in a lonely wood and, while George, Julian and Timmy go off to find a farmhouse from which to buy food, Dick mends a puncture in his bicycle tyre. Dick and Anne hear shouting in the woods and Richard bursts into the clearing where they are camping and tells them that he must find Julian and Timmy as Rooky, a brute of a man who used to act as his father's bodyguard, is trying to kidnap him. Richard runs off in the direction taken by Julian and George, Anne climbs a tree in the hope that she will be able to see the others returning, and Dick continues to mend his puncture. Soon afterwards two men appear and, mistaking Dick for Richard Kent, drag him off. Anne is petrified and is still up the tree when the others return. She explains what she saw and tells Julian that the men mentioned Owl's Dene as the place they were heading for. Julian looks at the map and they discover an Owl's Hill and decide to cycle there at once in the hope that Owl's Dene is close by. They find Owl's Dene with its high walls and huge gates and manage to get into the grounds when the automatic gates open. Once inside, they begin the search for Dick but are captured by the owner, Mr Perton, who shuts them in an upper room for the night. Julian manages to get out of the room and explores the house, which he discovers is a refuge for escaped prisoners and the base where crimes are planned. He discovers where the mechanism that controls the gates is kept and even finds a secret room hidden behind a bookcase where an escaped prisoner is hidden. The following day, the children are allowed the run of the grounds but cannot get over the high walls or escape through the gates.

Eventually they hit upon a plan. Richard, who is the smallest of the boys, hides in the boot of a car just before it leaves the grounds and, when the car stops in a nearby town, jumps out and manages to reach a police station just ahead of the driver. Richard tells the police what has happened and they go to Owl's Dene.

Meanwhile, Dick, George, Anne and Timmy have hidden in the secret room, while Julian goes to the room where the gate-operating mechanism is. The police arrive and Julian manages to let them in through the gates. Mr Perton denies any knowledge of hiding escaped convicts but Julian shows them where the secret room is. The convict is recaptured and the rest of the gang are rounded up by the police.

Five Fall Into Adventure

FIVE FALL INTO ADVENTURE (9)
Kidnappings and burglaries

In which the Five first meet Jo, George is kidnapped, and they escape from a particularly bad lot of villains.

The Five have only two weeks of their holiday left to spend at Kirrin Cottage. Uncle Quentin and Aunt Fanny are going to Spain on holiday, leaving the children in the care of Joanna, the cook. But villains have their eyes on Uncle Quentin's research work and, after they fail to steal the notebooks they want, they kidnap George in the hope that they can exchange her for the papers. The boys discover that Jo is partly involved in the kidnapping plot and she is persuaded to help them find George. They track the villains to their cliff-top hideout along the coast and enter through a tunnel that runs up through the cliff. There they encounter the near insane Red Tower and his henchmen, who have doped Timmy and are keeping George in the top room of the tower. Jo uses her amazing climbing skills to reach the tower room and takes George's place temporarily in order to fool the crooks, before turning the tables on them and locking Red and two other crooks in one of the tower rooms and running off with the key. The Five and Jo escape down the tunnel, row home and give the police the key to the room where the crooks have been safely locked!

FIVE ON A HIKE TOGETHER (10)
Out on the moors again

A half-term hike over the moors turns into a hunt for stolen jewels.

During the October half-term the Five go for a hike over the moors close to their schools. Timmy hurts one of his legs while scrambling down a rabbit hole and while Julian and George take him to get treatment, Dick and Anne continue on to Blue Pond Farm, where they intend to spend the night. Unfortunately they are given wrong directions to the farm and end up at a tumbledown cottage, where Dick spends a sleepless night in an old shed. During the night someone taps on the window,

Five On A Hike Together

whispers a strange message to him and slips a piece of paper through the broken window-pane.

The next day, when the Five are reunited, Dick tells them of the strange message and shows them the paper, which has a number of lines and words marked on it. Believing that all this may have something to do with a convict who has escaped from the prison on the moor, the children take the paper and their strange story to a local policeman, who disbelieves them and sends them on their way. As the police will not believe that their information is important, they decide to solve the mystery themselves. They think that the message came from Nailer, a criminal still in prison, who stole valuable jewels that have never been recovered. They set off for Two Trees, the large ruined house mentioned on the paper, where they meet Dirty Dick and Maggie, two disreputable characters who try to make the Five leave Two Trees. Timmy is able to protect the children and the race is on to find the stolen jewels.

One of the clues is 'Saucy Jane', which the Five believe refers to a boat, but when they look in the old boathouse next to the two trees the house takes its name from, they can't find a boat of that name and decide to search the lake, Gloomy Water, instead. They take out an old raft and suddenly realise that all the clues on the paper refer to landmarks that can be seen from the lake. At the point on the lake where the landmarks mentioned can all be seen at once Julian dives into the water, sees the Saucy Jane and feels that there is a large, waterproof sack wedged at one end of the boat. Unfortunately Dirty Dick and Maggie are also on the lake searching, so the Five decide to return after dark and recover the jewels by moonlight. They pull up the bag and find a fortune in stolen jewels hidden inside. These they carefully pack into their ruck-sacks and, early the next morning, take to the police. Maggie and Dirty Dick discover the sack and, realising that the Five have beaten them to the jewels, try to cut them off, but end up becoming trapped in a marsh. The Five telephone Mr Gaston, the man who had tended Timmy's leg, and he comes in his car and takes them to the police station, where they show the amazed inspector the jewels they have found.

They are given a lift back to their schools in a police car after having a very exciting half-term.

FIVE HAVE A WONDERFUL TIME (11)
Another caravan holiday

Faynights Castle, the return of Jo and the talents of the fair folk make this an exciting and entertaining adventure for the Five. Did they see a face in the tower room window - and has it got anything to do with a missing scientist?

Five Have A Wonderful Time

The Five are spending their Easter holiday in two old-fashioned caravans at Faynights Field, close to the ruined Faynights Castle. The fair folk arrive on the field and with them is Jo, whom the Five first met in *Five Fall Into Adventure*. While looking through George's binoculars, Dick and Julian believe they see a face at the window of the tower room in the castle. They investigate but find the tower entrance is blocked by fallen masonry. Later Timmy, who was made to stay outside the castle, appears in the courtyard and, when the children look to see how he found his way in, they discover the entrance to a secret passage running through the hollow wall of the castle. They decide to return after dark and explore the passage. The Five and Jo explore that night and discover a passage and stairs in the hollow of the castle leading to the tower room. Here they find Derek Terry-Kane, a missing scientist, being held prisoner. He has been imprisoned by Jeffrey Pottersham, another scientist, who wants to sell their secret research to a foreign power. Before they can escape, they hear a noise and Jo goes to investigate. Pottersham and his men have arrived and the Five are locked in the tower room. Jo is found, tied up and left in a little room off the secret passage but, with the aid of an ancient rusty dagger she finds in the room, she manages to escape, and returns to the camp-site to enlist the help of the fair folk in rescuing the Five and Derek Terry-Kane from the tower. Jo releases Beauty, one of the fair-folk's pythons, into the tunnel entrance, where he corners Pottersham who, in the dark, believes that there are dozens of huge snakes writhing around! The villains are captured and taken back to camp, where the fair folk remember they have another prisoner in one of the caravans. This turns out to be Uncle Quentin, who had been captured by mistake when he arrived at the camp looking for the Five. He is most annoyed, but calms down when he hears that the missing scientist has been found.

FIVE GO DOWN TO THE SEA (12)
Holiday on the Cornish coast

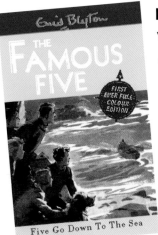

Five Go Down To The Sea

Fun in Cornwall as the Five explore the Wreckers' Tower, laugh at the antics of Clopper the horse and help track down a smuggler.

Summer holidays at Tremannon Farm with the farmer, Mr Penruthlan, and his wife. The Five meet Yan, and his grandad, the old shepherd, who tells them of the Wreckers' Tower and insists that on wild nights a light still shines from the tower-room. The Barnies, a troupe of travelling players, arrive at the farm, and prepare to give their show starring Clopper, the pantomime horse with the comical head. On the first stormy night, Julian and Dick go out to look for the light and see a man they believe to be Mr Penruthlan walking over the fields. The Five go to explore the Wreckers' Tower and find signs that someone had been signalling from the tower. They discover a secret passage leading to an old store-room once used by wreckers, but are trapped when someone locks and bolts the door. They are rescued by Yan, who takes them through the Wreckers' Way

108

which they discover ends under a trapdoor in an old shed on Tremannon Farm.

The Five find that Mr Penruthlan is actually working for the police and they tell him all they know. Whilst going over the events of the day Julian suddenly remembers that he has seen the Guv'nor acting suspiciously and realises that he is probably behind the smuggling. He tells Mr Penruthlan who says he will fetch the police to search the Barnies' wagons for the smuggled drugs. Meanwhile Dick becomes suspicious that the Guv'nor never leaves Clopper's head unguarded. He snatches Clopper's head, runs off with it and gives it to Mr Penruthlan, who discovers a secret compartment. Inside is a packet of smuggled drugs. The Guv'nor is locked up in a barn to await the arrival of the police and the Five enjoy a huge meal.

FIVE GO TO MYSTERY MOOR (13)
A moorland riding holiday

Mystery Moor with its sea mists and secrets places is the very place for the Five to uncover another adventure.

Five Go To Mystery Moor

The Five end up spending part of their Easter holiday at Captain Johnson's riding school, where they meet up with Henrietta, a tomboy who likes to be called Henry, William, a young guest at the school, and the gypsy-boy Sniffer and his dog, Liz. They learn about the history of Mystery Moor from old Ben, the blacksmith, and decide to explore part of it. They find and follow the old railway track and camp for the night in the old sand quarry, close to where Sniffer, his father and other gypsies are camped. That night the Five see a light set up in a hollow and hear a plane flying low overhead. When they investigate, they are amazed to discover that the plane is dropping packets containing American one-hundred-dollar bills.

They gather up the packets and Julian decides to hide them from the gypsies in the chimney of an ancient steam engine that once ran on the old railway track. A thick sea mist blows in, making it almost impossible to see where they are going, so the girls stay behind while the boys follow the railway track back to where the old engine lies half hidden in a gorse bush. In the mist, the boys are unable to find their way back to the girls. Worse still, the gipsies are on the track of the missing packages. Poor Timmy is cudgelled by Sniffer's father, and the two girls are captured, tied-up, and left in a cave in the middle of a hill. Sniffer, despite being terrified of his father, helps the girls. He brings the dazed Timmy to them and George sends her dog back to the riding school with a note fastened to his collar. Henry and William follow Timmy back and rescue the two girls. Meanwhile Julian and Dick have followed the railway track back to the riding school and arrive just as Henry and William return with George and Anne. The police are sent for, Julian explains about the aeroplane and the mysterious packages, and the gang is rounded up.

FIVE HAVE PLENTY OF FUN (14)
Back to Kirrin for the summer

Five Have Plenty Of Fun

A frightened young visitor at Kirrin Cottage, a transformation and a kidnapping bring the Five and Jo headlong into another adventure.

The Five are back at Kirrin Cottage again but George feels that things will be spoilt after the arrival of Berta and her dog, Sally. Berta's father is working on a secret project with Uncle Quentin, but evil men have threatened to kidnap her if he does not hand over the secrets. Berta is sent to Kirrin Cottage for safety and to confuse the kidnappers she is disguised as a boy, Lesley. With her hair cut short and wearing boys' clothes, the transformation is complete.

Uncle Quentin and Aunt Fanny have to leave Kirrin for a few days and, while they are away, the kidnappers mistake George for Berta and carry her off. In order to put the kidnappers further off the scent of the real Berta, the children decide to change her back into a girl again, rename her Jane and send her to live with Joan's cousin, who is looking after Ragamuffin Jo.

The police are informed of the kidnapping but Julian, Dick, Anne and Jo, who has cycled over to visit them, decide they will do a little investigation of their own. They follow Timmy and find several clues indicating that George was carried off in a large, blue American car. They also find a piece of paper with the word 'Gringo' inscribed on it in George's handwriting. Jo knows of a Gringo's Fair and goes to question Spiky, a boy who works at the fair, who tells her that Gringo does own a large, blue American car. They all go over to the fair and try and look in Gringo's caravan. An old lady shoos them away, but not before they have seen George's dressing gown in the caravan.

Spiky tells the children that earlier Gringo had gone off with his car pulling the trailer, and they enlist the help of Jim, a boy who works at Kirrin Garage, to discover the direction taken by the car and trailer. As luck would have it, they manage to find out it went to a large house in the village of Twining. Leaving Anne and Jo behind at Kirrin Cottage, Julian and Dick decide to go and investigate. They get into the house through a disused cellar, lock most of the bedrom doors and find George a prisoner in the tank room. Before they can escape, however, they are discovered by two men and locked in with George. Timmy goes for the men and they return to their room and lock themselves in.

Meanwhile Jo, who was annoyed at being forbidden to take part in the evening's adventure, has disobeyed Julian and cycled over to the house where she frees George, Dick and Julian and they return home. The police are told the whole story and go off to arrest all those involved in the kidnapping plot. Berta persuades her father to let her stay at Kirrin with the others.

FIVE ON A SECRET TRAIL (15)
Camping on Kirrin Common

Five On A Secret Trail

The ruined cottage, the Roman camp and visitors in the night. Why is someone so keen to drive the Five away from the common, and what is under the stone slab?

George is annoyed with people for laughing at Timmy when he has to wear a large cardboard collar to stop him scratching, so takes him off with her to camp on a lonely stretch of Kirrin Common. Later Anne joins her, and the two girls meet a boy named Guy who is excavating the site of an ancient Roman camp. One night during a thunder storm the girls take shelter in a ruined cottage and, during a flash of lightning, Anne believes she sees a group of people standing outside the cottage. When Julian and Dick join them, they decide to investigate further. They hide in the upper part of the ruined cottage, where they overhear the villains - who have been trying to frighten the children out of the cottage - discussing important stolen blueprints that are hidden somewhere behind a stone slab. The Five discover the slab and, with the help of Harry, Guy's twin brother, they move it and find a tunnel. This eventually leads them to a bag which they believe contains the stolen blueprints. They discover another tunnel blocked with a roof-fall and, after clearing part of it, discover Jet and Guy, who is lying there with an injured ankle. He explains that the villains came to the site of the Roman camp and moved a stone slab over a large hole. When he tried to stop them, they got rough with him. The villains believed that the blueprints were in the tunnel on the other side of the roof-fall and left Guy there while they went to fetch tools to move the earth. Julian bandages Guy's ankle and, hauling the two dogs up tied round with the boys' shirts, they climb out of the hole. The villains return and, after they have climbed down into the hole, Julian removes their rope, leaving them trapped underground. The children return to Kirrin, where the stolen blueprints are discovered in the lining of the bag and the police go off to rescue the villains from their underground prison.

FIVE GO TO BILLYCOCK HILL (16)
Another camping holiday

A secret airfield, the Billycock Caves and stolen aeroplanes are all part of the adventure when the Five go on a camping holiday to Billycock Hill

Five Go To Billycock Hill

The Five are camping on Billycock Hill close to the farm where Toby, a school friend of Julian's and Dick's, lives. They visit the butterfly farm where they meet the eccentric Mr Gringle, look down on the experimental airfield where Toby's cousin, Jeff, is a Flight-Lieutenant, and explore part of the Billycock Caves, where they see some spectacular stalagmites and stalactites.

One stormy night two of the experimental aircraft are stolen from the airfield and Jeff and his fellow pilot, Ray, disappear. Is Jeff a traitor who has stolen the aircraft to sell to a foreign government? Toby and the children find that difficult to believe and set out to uncover the truth. They do some detective work and discover that Will Janes, who once worked on Toby's farm and now lives with his old mother at the butterfly farm, knows something about the stolen planes and the police find out from him that foreign agents have persuaded him to help with the theft. Ray and Jeff have been kidnapped and imprisoned, but Will Janes doesn't know where they are being held. Everyone searches but the two pilots cannot be found. Later, Benny and Curly go missing and, after a big search, Benny is found close to the entrance to the Billycock Caves. He says that Curly has 'runned away' into the caves and, when later the piglet appears, the Five find a smudgy message written on his back. It says: 'Jeff Thomas and Ray Wells. Caves.' A search of the caves reveals the two pilots imprisoned down a hole in the cave floor. They are released and everyone goes back to the farm for a good feed. Jeff promises them all that he will arrange for them to have a flight in a plane at the airfield as soon as possible.

FIVE GET INTO A FIX (17)
A holiday in the Welsh mountains

Five Get Into A Fix

A winter holiday in the Welsh mountains. What causes the strange rumblings and the mysterious mist that hangs over Old Towers Hill, and why has nobody seen old Mrs Thomas for so long?

After suffering bad colds the Five go to recuperate in the Welsh mountains, where they stay in the Chalet on the mountainside at Magga Glen Farm. But the nights are disturbed by mysterious rumblings and vibrations and they see a strange-coloured mist hanging over Old Tower Hill. With the help of Aily, a wild-looking little girl who roams the mountainside with her pet lamb, Fany, and her dog, Dave, the Five investigate. They toboggan close to Old Tower Hill and Aily shows them a secret way into the house through a hole in the ground that leads down into the cellars. The children discover that old Mrs Thomas, who lives in the house, has been locked in her room and believes that her son, Llewellyn, has been killed after she refused to sell the house. Back in the cellars, the children discover an underground river running down through the hill. Fany gambols off down the river tunnel and Aily runs after her. George sends Timmy to bring her back but, when he too fails to return, the children all go to see what has happened. They discover that someone has been mining a rare mineral from the heart of the hill and transporting it down the underground river on large rafts. Suddenly they see Morgan and Aily's father walking up the tunnel alongside the underground river from the direction of the sea. They hide, believing that the two men are responsible for the illegal mining, but Morgan sees them. He angrily tells them off for interfering, and says that they must all hide quickly before they are discovered by the miners. But they are too late and the real miners, led by Llewellyn Thomas, capture them and tie Morgan's hands. With a great roar, Morgan shakes himself free and with his hands still tied, wades to the entrance of the tunnel leading to the sea where, with his mighty voice he repeatedly calls the names of his seven dogs. Suddenly there is a far off noise which grows louder as the seven dogs race up the tunnel alongside the underground river and, with the aid of Timmy, attack the miners. Morgans sends the children back to the farm while he sees to the arrest of the villains. The Five apologise to Morgan, whom they find was working for the police, and they help him to celebrate his birthday with a big feast.

FIVE ON FINNISTON FARM (18)
Summer holiday in Dorset

A holiday on Finniston Farm and stories of the long lost Finniston Castle. Can the Five discover the castle site and uncover its secrets before Mr Henning and Junior?

Five On Finniston Farm

The Five are staying at Finniston Farm in Dorset with Mr and Mrs Philpot and their twins, Harry and Harriet. The other guests at the farm are Mr Henning, an American anxious to buy up as many antiques as possible, and his obnoxious son, Junior. The Five hear of Finniston Castle, burned down in Norman times and its location forgotten. With the help of Henry and Harriet the Five decide to try and locate the castle site in the hope that they may find hidden treasure, but Junior overhears their plans and reports back to his 'Pop' who is also anxious to

115

find anything of value in the castle cellars and who obtains permission for a team of men with bulldozers to dig on what he believes is the castle site. The Five learn that a secret passage once linked the castle to the old chapel, which still stands and is now used as a storehouse on the farm. While searching for the passage, the children are accompanied not only by Timmy, but also by Snippet, the twins' poodle, and Nosey, a tame jackdaw. The twins order the dog to drop the bird, which at once scuttles off down a rabbit hole for safety. Snippet follows down the hole and it is a long time before the two animals return. When they do, Snippet carries an ancient dagger in his mouth and Nosey has a ring with a red stone in it in his beak. Excited that they seem to be on the track of treasure, the children begin digging and break through into the secret passage. They follow it to the castle cellars where they find armour, swords and a hoard of gold coins. They take a sword and some of the gold coins back with them to show the farmer and his wife, but on returning discover that there has been a roof-fall and they are trapped underground. Timmy leads them up the passage in the opposite direction and they discover the tunnel entrance leading up into the old chapel. They show the treasures they have found to Mr and Mrs Philpot and Great-Grandad and Mr Henning has his cheque returned. When the American begins to argue, Great-Grandad swings the sword around his head and all but chases the American and his son off the farm.

Five Go To Demon's Rocks

FIVE GO TO DEMON'S ROCKS (19)
Easter-time in a lighthouse

April at Demon's Rocks Lighthouse with crashing waves and stories of old-time wreckers. Is the wreckers' treasure really hidden near the rocks and, if so, can the Five find it?

Tinker Hayling, the nine year old son of Professor Hayling, comes to stay at Kirrin Cottage with his pet monkey, Mischief, while his father and Uncle Quentin discuss important work. But the noise of all the children and the two animals eventually becomes too much for the scientists, and Tinker hits upon the idea of taking the Five to stay in the lighthouse he owns at Demon's Rocks. They meet old Jeremiah Boogle who tells them stories of old-time wreckers who once lived near Demon's Rocks and who were supposed to have hidden a great fortune in gold, silver and pearls somewhere near the Wreckers' Cave. Jeremiah takes them to visit the cave and Mischief scampers off into one of the many tunnels that run through the cliffs. When the monkey returns he is grasping a gold coin in his paw. The Five and Tinker decide to search for the treasure but, before they can get started, Jacob and Ebby, descendants of one of the old-time wreckers and keen searchers for the lost treasure, lock them in the lighthouse. In a bid to escape, Julian and Dick decide to investigate the tunnel that runs through the foundations of the lighthouse. They hope that it joins a natural passage that might offer a way of escape. The boys go down into the foundations and find that the tunnel does lead into a passage and, while exploring, discover the hoard of gold and treasure. However, Jacob and Ebby are lying in wait for them and the boys only just manage to make it back up the tunnel to the lighthouse without being caught by the two wreckers or cut off by the tide which sweeps up through the tunnels. They show the others their finds and are determined to get out of the locked lighthouse. They try to signal with a table-cloth but that fails, so they light the great lamp and hang up the large bell used to warn ships in fog. When these are seen and heard in the village, Jeremiah and Constable Sharp come to investigate and break open the locked lighthouse door. The children tell them of their discovery and the boys show them where the treasure is hidden. After such an exciting adventure, the Five are more than glad to return to Kirrin Cottage.

FIVE HAVE A MYSTERY TO SOLVE (20)
Easter at Hill Cottage

Five Have A Mystery To Solve

The great harbour and mysterious Whispering Island. Why are guards still on the island and where is the legendary treasure hidden?

The Five go to stay at Hill Cottage to keep Wilfrid, the grandson of Mrs Layman, company. The cottage overlooks a great harbour with a large, tree-covered island in its centre. The children visit the local golf course and speak to old Lucas, the groundsman, who tells them the story of Whispering Island and the legendary treasures that were once supposed to have been taken there. Now watchmen patrol the island shore to stop boats landing there and to keep away tourists.

The Five hire a boat to row round the harbour but it is carried to the island by a strong tide and they decide to do a little exploring. But things begin to get rather *too* exciting when their boat is swept away and one of the island watchmen shoots at Timmy. They explore the woods and discover beautiful statues amongst the trees and a large shed with statues packed carefully inside long boxes. They decide that the statues are being smuggled out of the country to where they can be sold for large sums of money. They find an old well with a small, secret doorway halfway down the shaft and when Dick manages to open this he discovers more hidden statues. The Five believe that the doorway must be a secret opening into the place where all the castle treasures are hidden. Just then Timmy begins to bark and they find that Wilfred, hearing that their boat had been found drifting in the harbour, has hired a boat and rowed across to the island after them. They eventually find a passage up through the cliffs to a chamber where the statues and other treasures are stored, but two men arrive and the children try to hide. Unfortunately one of the men sees a movement and the children are discovered and locked in the cellar. Anne remembers the small door in the side of the well and they soon find it high up on one of the cellar walls. They pile up boxes to reach the door and begin to climb through and up the well-rope but when Dick tries to persuade George to go she refuses, preferring to remain behind with Timmy until he can find a way to escape. Just then one of the men returns and Timmy springs on him and knocks him out. Dick scrambles out of the door and up the well-rope while George and Timmy rush off up the passage back to the cliffs. They all row back to shore thinking of the exciting story they have to tell to the police of the treasure chamber and hidden statues.

FIVE ARE TOGETHER AGAIN (21)
A circus mystery

Camping with the circus, fun with Charlie the chimp and stolen plans. Can the Five track down Professor Hayling's stolen papers and can they prevent the thief from striking again?

Five Are Together Again

The Five go to stay at Big Hollow House with Professor Hayling, his son, Tinker, and Mischief, Tinker's pet monkey. Tapper's Circus comes to camp in the field at the end of Tinker's garden and the children have fun watching the circus acts, talking with the circus folk and getting to know Charlie the chimp and his owner, Mr Wooh.

Professor Hayling, who conducts some of his experiments in a tower built in the garden of Big Hollow House, has some of his top-secret papers stolen from the locked room at the top of the tower. All three doors into the tower room are still locked and the children are puzzled as to how the theft was committed. They are also determined that the Professor will not lose the rest of his secret papers. They plan that George will row over to Kirrin Island and hide the genuine papers while they make false ones to leave in their place for the thief to find. Timmy growls and they find Mr Wooh outside their tent. The children believe he may have overheard their plans and Julian annoys George by deciding that, as there could be danger, he will take the papers to Kirrin Island that night instead. The Five spend the rest of the day looking round the circus camp for a ladder to reach the tower room with, but are unable to find any long enough. Late that night when Julian prepares to take the papers to Kirrin Island he finds that George has already taken them. He and Dick race off on their bikes in the hope of overtaking her. When George reaches Kirrin Bay she is annoyed to see a light shining from Kirrin Island and, realising that there might be danger there, hides the precious papers in one of the fishing boats on the shore. She rows across to the island, hides her own boat and sets adrift another boat she finds there. Creeping up the beach she sees Mr Wooh and another man discussing the stolen papers. Mr Wooh is the thief and has overheard the children's plans. When the two villains are looking for their boat, George and Timmy manage to push them both into the sea before rowing back to Kirrin where they meet Julian and Dick. George explains that the villains are soaking wet and trapped on the island and they all return to Big Hollow House, taking the genuine papers with them. Next day the Five find a small clock in Charlie the chimp's cage. It is the one that went missing from the tower room at the same time as the papers. They realise that Mr Wooh, Charlie's owner, made the chimp climb up the wall of the tower and steal the papers. Charlie is sad that Mr Wooh is not around, but the children are sure that Jeremy Tapper, whom Charlie adores, will look after the chimp and give him a good home.

FIVE HAVE A PUZZLING TIME AND OTHER STORIES
A short story collection

A Lazy Afternoon

The Five are having a lazy afternoon in a shady copse close to Kirrin Cottage. A motorbike and sidecar turn off the road and enter the copse. The Five watch as two men climb a tree and hide a bag in its hollow trunk. Police arrive on motorbikes, arrest the men, Jim and Stan, and take away the bag.

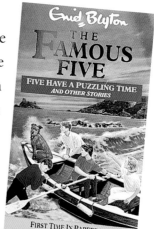

George's Hair Is Too Long

On their way to Windy Cove, the Five stop in Kirrin Village for George to get her hair cut. The hairdresser is closed for lunch so George goes to the ironmonger's to ask Mr Pails if she can borrow a pair of scissors to cut her own hair. Two men come into the shop, shut Geoge and Mr Pails in a cupboard, steal the safe and drive off in a van. Julian and the others, who have continued on their way to the cove, see the van race round a corner at break-neck speed and later find that it has burst a tyre. Anne notices the safe in the back of the van and, using a stick to write in the dust, tells Julian of her discovery. Meanwhile Timmy has returned to the village and found George. His barking alerts a man who releases the pair. George goes with Timmy, who finds the others by the van and recognises the two men as the safe robbers. They stop a passing car and, with the aid of the men in the car, take the robbers back to Kirrin in their stolen van.

Five And A Half-Term Adventure

One half-term the Five walk to Windy Hill, but as Julian's watch has stopped they find that it is getting dark without leaving them enough time to walk home. They go to Beckton and get a train back to Kirrin. In their compartment are a couple who have a baby so wrapped up in blankets that not even its face can be seen. Timmy is very interested in the baby and tries to jump up at it, which is very unusual behaviour for him. The Five later hear that a valuable dog has been stolen from the dog show in Beckton and realise that the supposed baby was actually the stolen dog. They inform the police and the couple are found with the dog in their cottage at Seagreen.

When Timmy Chased The Cat

Walking to Beckton, the Five pass Tarley's Mount, a large, isolated house. Timmy chases the cat there and, when they go to find him, they see the daily woman who tells them that the owner and her niece are away. Later they discover that Timmy has lost his collar disc and go back to the grounds of Tarley's Mount to look for it. They hear a radio on inside the house and Dick climbs a tree and peeps through a window. He sees a woman on the ground. They go in through an open side-door to find that the owner has fallen and hurt her hip. Julian telephones for an ambulance.

Well Done, Famous Five

The Five are on Kirrin Hill having a picnic. With George's binoculars they see some racehorses being exercised in the distance. Suddenly one off them is frightened by a fox and bolts. They follow the horse with their binoculars and see it go into a field. Dick cycles to the field to calm the horse down, while the others go for the police. Soon a horse-box arrives and the horse is taken back to its stable, none the worse for the experience.

Good Old Timmy

The Five go to bathe as Uncle Quentin is waiting for Professor Humes. On the beach they meet young Oliver Humes and see a couple of rough-looking men with a large mongrel dog. While they are swimming, the men seize Oliver and take him away in a car with their dog following along behind. Timmy follows the dog's trail and the Five find Oliver in a shed. Timmy draws the dog away while the Five rescue Oliver.

Happy Christmas, Five

It is Christmas Eve at Kirrin Cottage. Everyone has been doing up presents and filling a sack with them ready for next morning. Timmy gets excited and barks loudly, prompting Uncle Quentin to say he must go into his kennel for the night. Later George goes down and lets him in, but forgets to lock the door. Timmy hears a noise and barks. Uncle Quentin is furious that George has brought the dog into the house and sends him back out. But an intruder has sneaked in and is hiding in the cellar. When they are all back in bed and Timmy is in his kennel, Tom, the intruder, takes the sack of presents and hides it in a tumbledown shed. Timmy follows him and takes the presents back. Next morning Timmy presents the children with one of the gifts and they discover all the others in his kennel.

Five Have A Puzzling Time

George wakes in the night with terrible toothache and while looking out to sea spots a light on Kirrin Island. Next morning while she and Timmy go off to the dentist, Julian and the others row over to search the island, where one of Anne's sandals goes missing while she is paddling. Later all Five row over and find orange peel and grape stones scattered around. Then some of their chocolate biscuits disappear. They watch and see a monkey run out of a pile of seaweed. Behind the seaweed a boy, named Bobby Loman, and his dog, Chummy, are hiding. Bobby tells the Five that his grandfather has threatened to have his two pets put down. He goes back with the children to Kirrin Cottage where Aunt Fanny telephones the police and Bobby's grandfather. Bobby stays the night at Kirrin Cottage. After all the excitement, George finds that she has forgotten about the pain from her tooth.

QUIZ SECTION

Over 150 questions to test your knowledge of the Famous Five and their world. In all but the first section the number given in brackets refers to the Famous Five book in which the answer will be found. *Real* experts will be able to answer the questions without looking at the books - but if you're stuck, all the answers are listed at the end of this chapter!

Part One - Getting started
Half-a-dozen warm-up questions
to get the brain cells working!

1) Who wrote the adventures of the Famous Five?

2) Name the members of the Famous Five.

3) What is the name of the little island owned by one member of the Famous Five?

4) What sort of work does Uncle Quentin do?

5) What is the name of Uncle Quentin's wife and George's mother?

6) How many full-length books about the Famous Five did Enid Blyton write?

Part Two - Advanced questions for knowledgeable Famous Fivers.
Seven sections to really test your knowledge!

Section One: People

1) Who looked after Timothy for George when she was not allowed to keep him at Kirrin Cottage? (1)

2) Only one of the villains who goes to Kirrin Island to try and steal the gold ingots in the Five's first adventure is named. What is his name? (1)

3) Why is Pierre Lenoir known as 'Sooty' and why is his surname very appropriate? (4)

4) 'Tiger' Dan is one of the most unpleasant people the Five meet, yet from his job you would expect him to be a happy, jolly character. What does he do? (5)

5) Who owns the circus close to where the Five park their caravans in *Five Go Off In A Caravan?* (5)

6) Who goes camping with the Five in *Five Go Off to Camp?* (7)

7) Which of the Five thought they had been sitting near a volcano when camping on the moor? (7)

8) What job did Rooky do for Richard Kent's father? (8)

9) Why is Red Tower so named? (9)

10) Which female friend of the Five appears in three different Famous Five stories? (9/11/14)

11) Name the two crooks looking for stolen jewels at Two Trees. (10)

12) Name the kidnapped scientist in *Five Have A Wonderful Time.* (11)

13) Which human member of the Five is Jo most fond of? (9)

14) Name the two Barnies who operate Clopper, the pantomime horse. (12)

15) What is the name of the dirty, untidy, little character who follows the Five around when they are staying at Tremannon Farm? He lives with his old grandad, who is a shepherd. (12)

16) What is the name of the tomboy the Five meet at Captain Johnson's Riding School? (13)

17) Who were the family who ran the sand quarry on Mystery Moor, who disappeared suddenly and were never seen again? (13)

18) There are several sets of twins in the Famous Five books - which are the ones the Five meet excavating the old Roman camp on Kirrin Common? (15)

19) Who do the Five stay with when they visit Magga Glen Farm in

Wales? (17)

20) What is the name of the wild little girl who roams the Welsh mountainside with her pet lamb and dog? (17)

21) Who owns Old Towers? (17)

22) What is the name of the American boy staying at Finniston Farm? (18)

23) The name of the police constable at Demon's Rocks Village is a particularly good one for a policeman - what is it? (19)

24) Who tells the Five the story of the Demon's Rocks wreckers and also shows them round the Wreckers' Cave? (19)

25) By what name is Mr Tapper, owner of Tapper's Circus, know to the circus folk? (21)

Section Two: Know the word. Do you know the meaning of some of the interesting words Enid Blyton used in her Famous Five books?

1) What are ingots? (1)

2) Julian reads the Latin words 'via occulta' on an old piece of linen. What does he say he thinks the words mean? (2)

3) When Uncle Quentin is on Kirrin Island he signals to the children using heliography. What sort of signalling is heliography? (6)

4) While on the moor the Five go through Coney Copse and Julian explains that coney is a country word for something with which they are all very familiar – particularly Timmy! What does it mean? (10)

5) Throughout *Five Go To Mystery Moor* we hear of patrins. What are these? (13)

Section Three: Secret places and passages

1) Which two buildings does The Secret Way link? (2)

2) What name does Pierre Lenoir give to the network of passages that honeycomb Castaway Hill? (4)

3) Where does the secret passage that runs under the sea from Kirrin

Island go to? (6)

4) Who is the first of the Five to travel through the secret passage that runs under the sea from Kirrin Island to the mainland? (6)

5) Owl's Dene doesn't have a secret passage but it *does* have a secret room. What is this being used for when the Five visit? (8)

6) Near the end of the secret passage at Faynights Castle there is a small room with a shelf. Two articles are on the shelf, can you name either of them? (11)

7) The Five enter the Wreckers' Way from its secret entrance close to the beach. Where does it lead to? (12)

8) One entrance to the secret passage on Kirrin Common is found close to the spring of fresh water. Where does the passage lead? (15)

9) Which two places does the secret passage at Finniston Farm run between? (18)

10) What were the villains on Whispering Island taking along the secret passage that ran from the cellars of the castle to the coast? (20)

Section Four: Places

1) How many towers did Kirrin Castle have? (1)

2) In *Five Run Away Together,* where do the Five camp on Kirrin Island? (3)

3) What surrounds Castaway Hill?

4) Where is the old quarry at Kirrin? For a bonus mark, say how far away from Kirrin Cottage it is. (6)

5) What is the name of the disused railway yard looked after by 'Wooden Leg' Sam? (7)

6) Where is Dick taken after he is mistaken for Richard Kent and kidnapped? (8)

7) What is the name of the small lake close to Two Trees where the Five go to search for hidden jewels? (10)

8) What is the name of the castle close to where the Five stay in *Five Have A Wonderful Time*? (11)

9) In which county of England is *Five Go Down To The Sea* set? (12)

10) What is the name of the village close to Mystery Moor from where the old railway track ran? (13)

11) There is an ancient camp being excavated on Kirrin Common. Which period of history is it from? (15)

12) Where do the Five go to ski and toboggan after they have all had bad colds? One mark for the country and another for the actual farm or village. (17)

13) Lucas tells the children that Whispering Island had two other names. What are they? (20)

14) What is the name of the field owned by Professor Hayling, where Tapper's Circus camps? (21)

15) What is the name of the house where Tinker and Professor Hayling live? (21)

Section Five: The Five in action!

1) How did the Five open the old box they found in the wreck? (1)

2) How is Dick's cheek injured when they are trying to open the dungeon door at Kirrin Castle? (1)

3) When the Five are trapped in the tunnels under Merran Hills, how do they try to get out? (5)

4) Where does Julian hide when the others go into town and he stays behind to keep a lookout for Lou and Tiger Dan? (5)

5) When the children are trapped underground in *Five Go Off In A Caravan*, where does Dick go to telephone for help? (5)

6) What do the villains plan to do to Kirrin Island if Quentin Kirrin refuses to give them the results of his secret experiments? (6)

7) How does George try to find out when the boys are leaving their tent to go and look for spook trains in the middle of the night? (7)

8) How does Julian avoid being locked into the bedroom with the others at Owl's Dene? (8)

9) How does Richard Kent escape from Owl's Dene? (8)

10) Where is Anne hiding when Dick is kidnapped in *Five Get Into Trouble?* (8)

11) How does Jo get into the tower room to rescue George in *Five Fall Into Adventure?* (9)

12) How does Dick fool the kidnappers into thinking that he is still at Kirrin Cottage with the others when he wants to keep a lookout for the villains in *Five Fall Into Adventure?* (9)

13) When the Five are exploring the secret passage at Faynights Castle they find something on the floor that shows them other people have been along the passage recently. What is it they find? (11)

14) What clues do the Five find in the Wreckers' Tower that leads them to believe that someone has been there with an oil lamp? (12)

15) Who unlocks the door after the Five have been locked into the storeroom they discover along the secret passage from the Wreckers' Tower? (12)

16) Towards the end of *Five Go Down To The Sea,* Dick suddenly grabs Clopper's head and runs off with it. Why does he do this? (12)

17) Julian and Dick 'borrow' the costume for Clopper, the pantomime horse, and practice galloping in it. What happens when they try to remove the costume? (12)

18) Where do Julian and Dick hide the forged hundred-dollar bills they find on Mystery Moor? (13)

19) Who do Julian and Dick ask for help in finding Gringo's car and caravan after it leaves the fairground? (14)

20) How does Julian prevent the villains escaping from the underground cave on the site of the old Roman camp at Kirrin Cottage? (15)

21) How do the boys look into the upstairs room of the cottage at the butterfly farm? (16)

22) When the Five are locked in Demon's Rocks Lighthouse they use three different methods to signal for help. Can you name all three? (19)

23) Where did Dick discover one small entrance to the cellars of the castle-like house on Whispering Island? (20)

24) Where do the Five first decide to hide Professor Hayling's secret papers to prevent them from being stolen? (21)

25) When George sees a light on Kirrin Island she does not take the secret papers to the island. What does she do with them? (21)

Section Six: Animal antics – what do you know about the animals in the Famous Five stories?

1) Which animals does Timmy love chasing, particularly when he's on Kirrin Island? (1)

2) What was the trick Timmy wouldn't show Mr Roland when the Five took him to meet their tutor at Kirrin Station? (2)

3) What nickname does George give to the Stick's dog? An extra point for his real name! (3)

4) How do the children get Timmy down into the pit when they are staying at Smuggler's Top? (4)

5) What sort of animal is Pongo? (5)

6) What are the names of the ponies who pull the caravans in *Five Go Off In A Caravan?* (5)

7) What does Timmy carry back through the under-sea passage from Kirrin Island to the mainland? (6)

8) Who does Timmy bite when the Five are at Owl's Dene? (8)

9) While the Five are on their hike, Timmy hurts his leg. How does he do this? For a bonus point, name the man who looks at Timmy's injured leg. (10)

10) Beauty is the name of the snake that helps Jo scare the villains in *Five Have A Wonderful Time*. What sort of snake is he? (11)

11) Name any of the farm dogs to be found at Tremannon Farm. (12)

12) What sort of animals does Yan's grandad look after? (12)

13) Sniffer's dog, Liz, can do a number of tricks. Can you name two of them? (13)

14) What is the name of Sniffer's skewbald horse? (13)

15) What is the name of Berta Wright's little poodle? (14)

16) What is the name of Guy Lawdler's small dog - and a bonus point if you know what it's short for! (15)

17) What is the name of the piglet owned by Benny at Billycock Farm - and why is he called this? (16)

18) What other unusual pets has Benny had? (16)

19) How many dogs does Morgan Jones have? Can you name them all? (17)

20) What sort of a creature is Nosey at Finniston Farm? (18)

21) What breed of dog is Snippet? (18)

22) What does Timmy receive from Mischief as a peace offering? (19)

23) What did Mischief find when the Five and Tinker were in the Wreckers' Cave? (19)

24) What does Wilfrid use to entice shy wild animals to come to him? (20)

25) What is the name of the chimpanzee at Tapper's Circus? (21)

Section Seven: Transport – getting around with the Famous Five.

1) When they have luggage with them how do the Five usually travel from Kirrin Station to Kirrin Cottage? (2)

2) How do the Five get to Smuggler's Top? (4)

3) How many caravans do the Five have with them in *Five Go Off In A Caravan?* (5)

4) How is all the equipment carried when the Five and Mr Luffy go camping? (7)

5) How are the children travelling in *Five Get Into Trouble?* (8)

6) How are George and Timmy taken to Ravens Wood after they are kidnapped from Kirrin Cottage? (9)

7) How do the children and Jo get to the cliff-top hideout belonging to Red Tower? (9)

8) When the Five are at Gloomy Water what do they use to get out into the middle of the lake? (10)

9) At the end of *Five On A Hike Together*, how do the children get back to their schools? (10)

10) How do the travelling players known as The Barnies travel from village to village? (12)

11) How are the forged hundred-dollar bills delivered to Mystery Moor? (13)

12) How do the children travel across Mystery Moor when they are following Sniffer and his caravan? (13)

13) How was sand transported from the quarry on Mystery Moor to Milling Green? (13)

14) Gringo, the fair owner, has a big car. Which country does it come from? (14)

15) How was Berta Wright brought to Kirrin after her father thought she was in danger of being kidnapped? (14)

16) How did the boys and Jo travel to Gringo's house at Twining when they were looking for the kidnapped George? (14)

17) How do the Five carry their camping equipment up to Billycock Hill from the farm? (16)

18) What 'transport' do the Five and Aily use for the first part of their journey when they go to find the 'big hole' that Aily says will lead them into Old Towers? (17)

19) The Five meet at Finniston Village after arriving by two different means of transport. What were these? (18)

20) What was the name of the boat the Five hired when they stayed at Hill Cottage? (20)

Part Three – Mastermind questions for top-notch Famous Fivers!

1) Name Jennifer Armstrong's four dolls in *Five Run Away Together*. (3)

2) What is the real name of Lou the acrobat, encountered by the Five in *Five Go Off In A Caravan?* (5)

3) In which country did Tiger Dan work before joining Mr Gorgio's circus? (5)

4) What do the children go looking for in the old quarry on the moors behind Kirrin Cottage? (6)

5) What was the name of the farm where Jock Robins lived before he moved to Olly's Farm? (7)

6) What was the name of the pool where the Five and Mr Luffy swam when they were camping on the moors? (7)

7) What sort of car do the villains at Owl's Dene use? (8)

8) What were the children given for Christmas just before *Five Get Into Trouble* begins? (8)

9) Where are Uncle Quentin and Aunt Fanny going on holiday at the start of *Five Fall Into Adventure*? An extra point if you can name the city, as well as the country. (9)

10) Name the horse that Jo's father uses to pull his caravan. (9)

11) The Five find three boats in the boathouse at Gloomy Water. What are each of the boats named? (10)

12) Whose jewels are hidden in Gloomy Water? (10)

13) In *Five Have A Wonderful Time,* George is reminded that she has to send a birthday card to one of her relatives. Who is this relative, and when is her birthday? (11)

14) Skippy, the wife of Bufflo, plays a musical instrument. What is it? (11)

15) What is the name of the small railway station the Five get off at when they are going to stay at Tremannon Farm? (12)

16) How many brothers does Henry, the tomboy at Captain Johnson's riding school have? (13)

17) Why do the Five have to stay another week at Captain Johnson's riding school rather than return to Kirrin Cottage as originally planned? A bonus point if you can explain why they couldn't go to Julian, Dick and Anne's home instead. (13)

18) What are we told that Uncle Quentin once spread on his toast instead of marmalade? (14)

19) What is the name of the thief who stole the blueprints in *Five On A Secret Trail*? (15)

20) What is the name of the cat at Billycock Farm? His name is only mentioned once in the story. (16)

21) On their way to Billycock Hill the Five stop on top of a hill from which Julian says they can see a number of different counties. How many does he say they can see? (16)

22) Where do the Five get their water from when they are staying at the Chalet on Magga Glen Farm? (17)

23) In which Dorset town was the hotel where Mr Henning and Junior went for an evening meal? (18)

24) What was the name of the dog that Great-Grandad at Finniston Farm said he once owned? (18)

25) Professor Hayling has an old parchment giving his family the right to Cromwell's Corner Field for ever. What is the date on the parchment? (21)

Answers

Part One: Getting Started

1. Enid Blyton
2. George, Anne, Julian, Dick and Timmy the dog.
3. Kirrin Island. It is owned by George.
4. He is a scientist. He also writes scientific books and lectures on his work.
5. Aunt Fanny.
6. 21.

Part Two: Advanced

Section One: People

1. Alf, the fisherboy (a bonus point if you said Alf and James, as in some editions of the books he is given both names!).
2. Jake
3. He has very dark eyes, hair and eyebrows. In French, his surname Lenoir means 'the black one'.

4. He is the chief clown at the circus.

5. Mr Gorgio.

6. Mr Luffy, one of the teachers at the boys' school.

7. Anne.

8. He was his bodyguard.

9. Because of his bright red hair, beard and eyebrows.

10. Ragamuffin Jo.

11. Dirty Dick Taggart and Maggie Martin.

12. Derek Terry-Kane.

13. She is fond of Dick, who was kind to her at their first meeting.

14. Sid operates the back legs and Mr Binks operates the front and the head.

15. Yan.

16. Henrietta, who likes to be called Henry.

17. The Bartle family.

18. Guy and Harry Lawdler.

19. The Thomas family.

20. Aily.

21. Mrs Bronwen Thomas.

22. Junior Henning.

23. PC Sharp

24. Jeremiah Boogle

25. He is called 'Old Grandad'.

Section Two: Know the word

1. Blocks of metal. The ones the Five find are made of solid gold!

2. Secret Way.

3. Using the sun's rays and a mirror to flash a signal.

4. Coney is another word for rabbit.

5. Secret signs, often made from twigs or leaves, left by gypsies to give other gypsies a message.

Section Three: Secret places and passages

1. Kirrin Cottage and Kirrin Farmhouse.

2. The Catacombs.

3. The old quarry on the moors behind Kirrin Cottage.

4. Timmy.

5. To hide escaped convicts.

6. An old pitcher and a broken, rusty dagger are on the shelf.

7. To Tremannon Farm. It comes out in a machine shed.

8. It leads to the site of the ancient Roman camp on the common.

9. The cellars of the castle that once stood there, and the old chapel, now used as a grain store.

10. *They were smuggling treasures from the castle, mainly valuable statues.*

Section Four: Places

1. *Two.*
2. *In a cave they find on the shore near the old wreck.*
3. *Marshes.*
4. *The quarry is on the moor behind Kirrin Cottage. It is about quarter of a mile away from the cottage.*
5. *Olly's Yard.*
6. *Owl's Dene on Owl's Hill.*
7. *Gloomy Water.*
8. *Faynights Castle.*
9. *Cornwall.*
10. *Milling Green.*
11. *Roman times. It's an ancient Roman camp.*
12. *They go to Wales and stay at Magga Glen Farm in the village of Magga Glen.*
13. *Wailing Island and Keep-Away Island.*
14. *Cromwell's Corner.*
15. *Big Hollow House.*

Section Five: The Five in action

1. *They threw it out of an upstairs window at Kirrin Cottage on to the ground.*
2. *A long splinter of wood flies off the door and embeds itself in his cheek.*
3. *They try to wade down one of the underground streams which they hope will eventually come out of the side of the hill.*
4. *He hides on top of one of the caravans.*
5. *He goes to the farmhouse owned by Farmer Mackie.*
6. *They plan to blow up the entire island.*
7. *She ties one end of a length of thin string to their tent flaps and the other end to her big toe. Then, when the string is pulled it will wake her up!*
8. *He piles up a blanket to look like a sleeping person and then hides in a cupboard on the landing outside the bedroom.*
9. *He hides in the boot of the car when it is about to leave the house and then escapes after the car has stopped.*
10. *She has climbed to the top of a tree to keep a lookout for Julian and George.*
11. *She climbs up the ivy that covers the tower wall.*
12. *He borrows the jacket, cap and delivery bag belonging to Sid, the boy who delivers the evening paper to Kirrin Cottage.*
13. *They find chocolate wrappers on the floor.*
14. *They find a trail of spilt oil leading up the stairs to the tower room.*

15. *Yan unlocks and unbolts the door.*

16. *He believes that the smuggled goods might be hidden inside the head.*

17. *They cannot undo the zip that holds the two sections together!*

18. *In the funnel of the ancient steam engine that once carried sand from the quarry.*

19. *Jim the garage boy. He telephoned the boys working in garages in neighbouring towns to see if they had seen the caravan and car pass.*

20. *He removes the rope that they need to climb out of the cave.*

21. *They find a ladder, rest it against the wall, climb up and look in the window.*

22. *1) They try to hang a white tablecloth out of the window, but it blows away. 2) They light the great lamp at the top of the lighthouse. 3) They hang a large bell on the gallery outside the lamp room and ring it.*

23. *He discovered the entrance halfway down the well-shaft.*

24. *On Kirrin Island.*

25. *She hides them under the tarpaulin covering one of the fishermen's boats.*

Section Six: Animal antics

1. *Rabbits.*

2. *He refused to hold out his paw to shake hands.*

3. *George calls the dog Stinker. His real name is Tinker.*

4. *They lower him down in a laundry basket tied to a strong rope.*

5. *He's a chimpanzee.*

6. *Dobby and Trotter.*

7. *Uncle Quentin's notebook, with all the information on his secret formula in it.*

8. *Rooky.*

9. *Timmy hurts his leg after he gets stuck down a rabbit hole and has to be pulled out. Mr Gaston looks at his leg.*

10. *Beauty is a python.*

11. *Ben (or Bennie), Bouncer, Nellie and Willie.*

12. *Sheep. He is a shepherd.*

13. *She can walk on her hind legs and do forward rolls.*

14. *Clip.*

15. *Sally.*

16. *Jet – short for Jet Propelled.*

17. *Curly – because of his curly tail.*

18. *A lamb and two goslings.*

19. *He has seven dogs. Their names are: Dai, Bob, Tang, Doon, Joll, Rafe and Hal.*

20. *A tame jackdaw.*

21. *He is a poodle.*

22. *A biscuit.*

23. *A gold coin.*

24. *He plays a soft, sad tune on his little wooden flute.*

25. *Charlie the chimp.*

Section Seven: Transport

1. *In a pony trap.*

2. *They travel in a hired car.*

3. *Two caravans.*

4. *In a trailer pulled by Mr Luffy's car*

5. *On bikes. They are on a cycling holiday..*

6. *They are taken in Simmy's caravan.*

7. *They sail there in George's boat and then go up the hidden passageway through the cliff to the house.*

8. *A raft.*

9. *They get a ride back in a police car.*

10. *In old-fashioned open wagons.*

11. *They are dropped by low-flying aircraft.*

12. *They ride on horseback.*

13. *It was transported in wagons along a railway track pulled by a steam engine.*

14. *America.*

15. *She came in a boat, which made her feel sea-sick.*

16. *They went on their bicycles. Jo 'borrowed' Anne's bike.*

17. *They push it up in a handcart.*

18. *They go on their toboggans.*

19. *The girls and Timmy went by bus, while the two boys cycled.*

20. *It was called 'Adventure'.*

Part Three: Mastermind

1. *Josephine, Angela, Rosebud and Marigold.*

2. *Louis Allburg.*

3. *Holland.*

4. *Flint arrowheads and other prehistoric flint tools.*

5. *Owl's Farm.*

6. *The Green Pool.*

7. *A Bentley.*

8. *Two small tents.*

9. *They go to Seville in Spain.*

10. *The horse is called Blackie.*

11. *Merry Meg, Cheeky Charlie and Careful Carrie.*

12. *The Queen of Fallonia.*

13. *Her grandmother. Her birthday is in April.*

14. *She plays the guitar.*

15. *Polwilly Halt.*

16. *Three.*

17. *1) Because Uncle Quentin is ill. 2) Julian, Dick and Anne's parents are abroad and their house is being decorated.*

18. *Mustard.*

19. *Paul.*

20. *Tinky.*

21. *Five.*

22. *They boil snow.*

23. *Dorchester.*

24. *True.*

25. *1648.*

CHAPTER ELEVEN

COLLECTING THE FAMOUS FIVE

Ever since the first book in the series was published, children and adults have been collecting Famous Five books and games. You may not be able to afford first editions but, if you keep your eyes open at school fairs, jumble sales and car-boot sales, you could be lucky enough to find interesting Famous Five collectables at bargain prices. This section will help you know what to look out for.

Books and annuals

For over twenty years the Famous Five books were only published as hardback books with colourful paper jackets. Millions of copies were sold and they can still often be found in second-hand bookshops. The first Famous Five paperbacks were published in 1967. These had the lovely Eileen Soper illustrations inside but an artist named Betty Maxey had illustrated the new covers. In 1974 Betty Maxey also reillustrated the insides of all the books. Some collectors like to have books illustrated by both artists in their collections.

If you like annual-sized books, look out for the ten Famous Five Annuals published between 1977 and 1996. Most contained a complete Famous Five story as well as other interesting features. I have managed to find all of mine at jumble sales. Harder to find are the four *Enid Blyton's Magazine Annuals*, each of which contained a Famous Five short story.

Another series of large books to look out for are the three Famous Five Cartoon Books published by Hodder & Stoughton in 1983 and 1984. Each book contained a complete Famous Five adventure in colour comic strip form. A complete list of the Famous Five Annuals and large books can be found in Appendix 4 at the back of this book.

Magazines and comics

Famous Five stories and picture strips have appeared in many magazines and comics. *Sunny Stories* and *Enid Blyton's Magazine* are hard to find but others, like *Look In, Enid Blyton's Mystery and Suspense* and *Enid Blyton's Adventure Magazine* can still often be found at school fairs. Look out particularly for the three *Look In* magazines that had the Famous Five on their covers. There is a complete list of these magazines in Appendix 2 at the back of this book.

Games

In 1951 a firm called Pepys published a Famous Five card game. There were 44 coloured cards in the set and each one showed a character or scene from a Famous Five adventure. In 1978 the cards were redrawn to look like the actors who played the Five in the television series.

The same firm published two Famous Five Party Games called *What's Wrong*. Each card showed a scene from a Famous Five adventure with nine mistakes for players to spot.

When the 1978 TV series was being broadcast Whitman brought out a big, boxed game called *Enid Blyton's Famous Five Kirrin Island Treasure Quest Game*. It is now very rare to find this game complete.

Much easier to find is the series of Famous Five Adventure Game books published by Hodder & Stoughton during the 1980s. There were eight in the set and each one was based on a Famous Five adventure. Each game book came in a plastic

wallet with a dice, map and games cards. If you find one of these at a jumble sale, check that the dice and cards are still with it!

Puzzles

The very first Famous Five puzzle was published in 1955 by a firm called Bestime. They eventually brought out twenty different Famous Five jigsaw puzzles, each one painted by Eileen Soper, who illustrated the Famous Five books. You will be very fortunate to find one of these as they are now very scarce indeed. A list appears in Appendix 5.

Easier to find are the series of jigsaw puzzles published in 1975 by Whitman. In 1978 the same firm brought out another series showing scenes from the Famous Five TV series. The most recent Famous Five jigsaw puzzle was published by Paul Lamond Games in 1991. It showed the Five going down into the old wreck.

Other collectables

Over the years there have been many other Famous Five collectables. Some are listed here, though you might be able to add to the list!

Famous Five Club badge, bookmark and membership card (1953-1990).

Famous Five writing paper and envelope set in colourful box (1950s).

Famous Five windcheater and sweater (1950s).

Famous Five birthday cards (1950s).

Famous Five postcard (sent out by Enid Blyton to children who wrote to her).

Sculptorcraft Famous Five moulds (1950s/60s).

Programmes and posters to the Famous Five stage plays (1950s/1990s).

Famous Five colouring and puzzle books based on the 1978 TV series.

Famous Five lunch-box (1978).

Tapes and records of Famous Five stories (1970s-2000).

Appendix I

PUBLICATION DATES OF THE FAMOUS FIVE BOOKS

The twenty one Famous Five novels were all originally published by Hodder & Stoughton as hardback books with dustwrappers.

	Title	Publisher	First edition date
1	*Five On A Treasure Island*	Hodder & Stoughton	Sept 1942
2	*Five Go Adventuring Again*	Hodder & Stoughton	July 1943
3	*Five Run Away Together*	Hodder & Stoughton	Oct 1944
4	*Five Go To Smuggler's Top*	Hodder & Stoughton	Oct 1945
5	*Five Go Off In A Caravan*	Hodder & Stoughton	Nov 1946
6	*Five On Kirrin Island Again*	Hodder & Stoughton	Oct 1947
7	*Five Go Off To Camp*	Hodder & Stoughton	Oct 1948
8	*Five Get Into Trouble*	Hodder & Stoughton	Oct 1949
9	*Five Fall Into Adventure*	Hodder & Stoughton	Sept 1950
10	*Five On A Hike Together*	Hodder & Stoughton	Sept 1951
11	*Five Have A Wonderful Time*	Hodder & Stoughton	Sept 1952
12	*Five Go Down To The Sea*	Hodder & Stoughton	Sept 1953
13	*Five Go To Mystery Moor*	Hodder & Stoughton	July 1954
14	*Five Have Plenty Of Fun*	Hodder & Stoughton	July 1955
15	*Five On A Secret Trail*	Hodder & Stoughton	July 1956
16	*Five Go To Billycock Hill*	Hodder & Stoughton	July 1957
17	*Five Get Into A Fix*	Hodder & Stoughton	July 1958
18	*Five On Finniston Farm*	Hodder & Stoughton	July 1960
19	*Five Go To Demon's Rocks*	Hodder & Stoughton	July 1961
20	*Five Have A Mystery To Solve*	Hodder & Stoughton	July 1962
21	*Five Are Together Again*	Hodder & Stoughton	July 1963
	Five Have A Puzzling Time, And Other Stories	Red Fox	Oct 1995

Appendix 2

FAMOUS FIVE STORIES IN MAGAZINES AND COMICS

Sunny Stories (serial story)

Five Go Off To Camp no. 426 - no. 444, 19th March 1948 -
26th November 1948.

Enid Blyton's Magazine (serial story)

Five Go Down To The Sea Vol. 1 no.1 - Vol.1 no. 19, 18th March 1953 -
1st November 1953.
Five On A Secret Trail Vol. 3 no. 15 - Vol. 4 no. 8, 20th July 1955 -
9th May 1956.
Five Go To Billycock Hill Vol. 4 no.9 - Vol. 5 no. 5, 23rd May 1956 -
27th February 1957.
Five Get Into A Fix Vol. 5 no. 15 - Vol. 6 no. 10 17th July 1957 -
7th May 1958.

Princess comic (serial story)

Five At Finniston Farm (Five On Finniston Farm) 30th January 1960 -
4th June 1960.
Five Have A Puzzling Time (4-part short story*)* 20th August 1960 -
10th September 1960.
Five Go To Demon's Rock 14th January 1961 - 24th June 1961.
Five Together Again (*Five Are Together Again*) 26th January 1963 -
18th May 1961.

Look In

From 22nd July 1978, *Look In* serialized several of the Famous Five books
as black and white picture strips.

Enid Blyton's Adventure Magazine
(full length colour picture strip versions)
1985

No.1 *Five Go Down To The Sea*

No. 2 *Five Go Off To Camp*

No. 3 *Five On Finniston Farm*

No. 4 *Five On A Hike Together*

1986

No.5 *Five Get Into A Fix*

No. 6 *Five Go To Billycock Hill*

No. 7 *Five Go To Mystery Moor*

No. 8 *Five Have A Mystery To Solve*

No. 9 *Five Get Into Trouble*

No. 10 *Five Go To Smuggler's Top*

No. 11 *Five Have Plenty Of Fun*

No. 12 *Five On A Treasure Island*

No. 13 *Five Run Away Together*

No. 14 *Five Go To Demon's Rocks*

No. 15 *Five Go Adventuring Again*

No. 16 *Five Go Off In A Caravan*

Enid Blyton's Mystery and Suspense
(Serials/short story: colour picture strip)
1997

Five On A Treasure Island no. 1 – no. 6.

George's Hair Is Too Long no. 7.

Five Go To Smuggler's Top no. 8 – no.10.

Appendix 3

FAMOUS FIVE SHORT STORIES
First publication of all known Famous Five short stories.

Famous Five stories in *Enid Blyton's Magazine Annual*

Enid Blyton's Magazine Annual Number 1 (1954) "A Lazy Afternoon"
Enid Blyton's Magazine Annual Number 2 (1955) "George's Hair Is Too Long!"
Enid Blyton's Magazine Annual Number 3 (1956) "Five - And A Half-Term Adventure!"
Enid Blyton's Magazine Annual Number 4 (1957) "When Timmy Chased The Cat!"

Famous Five Story in *Wheaties* booklet (1956)

Well Done, Famous Five

Famous Five stories in *Princess Gift Book For Girls*

Princess Gift Book For Girls (1961) Good Old Timmy!
Princess Gift Book For Girls (1962) Happy Christmas, Five!

Note: All the above stories were reprinted in *Five Have A Puzzling Time And Other Stories* by Red Fox in 1995.

Appendix 4

FAMOUS FIVE ANNUALS AND LARGE BOOKS

The first nine annuals were published by Purnell and each one was made up of a complete Famous Five story told partly in picture strip and partly in text, together with features on camping, hiking, dungeons and reptiles. The tenth annual was published by Grandreams. It contained three short Famous Five stories as well as features and photographs.

Famous Five On A Hike Together	Purnell	September 1977
Famous Five Go Adventuring Again	Purnell	September 1978
Famous Five Go To Smuggler's Top	Purnell	September 1979
Five Go To Mystery Moor	Purnell	September 1980
Five Have A Wonderful Time	Purnell	September 1981
Five On Kirrin Island Again	Purnell	September 1982
Five Have A Mystery To Solve	Purnell	August 1983
Five Go Off To Camp	Purnell	August 1984
Five Go Down To The Sea	Purnell	August 1985
The Famous Five Annual	Grandreams	October 1996

In 1983 and 1984 Hodder & Stoughton published three Famous Five Cartoon Books. Each book contained a complete Famous Five adventure in picture strip form. Unfortunately these were not based on any of the Enid Blyton books, but on stories created by a French author named Claude Voilier, based on Enid Blyton's characters. The titles were:

The Famous Five and the Golden Galleon	1983
The Famous Five and the Inca God	1983
The Famous Five and the Treasure of the Templars	1984

Appendix 5

FAMOUS FIVE JIGSAW PUZZLES BY BESTIME

Produced mid-1950s to early 1960s, all with illustrations by Eileen Soper. Bestime published jigsaw puzzles of other Enid Blyton characters as well as the Famous Five. The first Famous Five jigsaw was puzzle number 29.

No.	Title
29	Five In Camp
30	Five In Smuggler's Cove
31	Five At The Circus
32	Five Go To Sea
41	Five Have A Moorland Picnic
42	Five On Kirrin Island
43	Five Help With Harvest
44	Five At The Airfield
45	Five On A Windy Day
46	Five Have A Wonderful Time
47	Five Fall Into Adventure
48	Five On A Holiday
53	Five In A Speedboat
54	Five Have Fun In Snow
55	Five Go Riding
56	Five Round A Campfire
65	Five In The Garden
66	The New Tractor
67	Five At The Zoo
68	Five On A Climbing Holiday

Appendix 6

ENGLISH LANGUAGE FAMOUS FIVE FILM AND TELEVISION PRODUCTIONS

There have been two cinema serials and two television series of the Famous Five. The cinema serials were made in black-and-white and both TV series in colour. Enid Blyton was very involved in the 1957 version of *Five On A Treasure Island* and auditioned the children who were to play Julian, George, Dick and Anne. The film was made in Dorset with Corfe Castle being used for Kirrin Castle.

1957

Five On A Treasure Island Produced for the Children's Film Foundation. Eight episodes, each running approximately 16 minutes. The serial was released on video in 1993.

1964

Five Have A Mystery To Solve Produced for the Children's Film Foundation. Six episodes, each running approximately 16 minutes.

1978/9

Southern Television series The Southern Television series ran over two seasons and consisted of twenty-six 25-minute episodes. Three of the books, *Five On A Treasure Island, Five Have A Mystery To Solve* and *Five Have Plenty Of Fun,* were not adapted for the series. Eight of the novels were adapted as two-parters. All episodes have been released on video.

Title	Running time
Five Go Adventuring Again	1 x 25 minutes
Five Run Away Together	1 x 25 minutes
Five Go To Smuggler's Top	2 x 25 minutes
Five Go Off In A Caravan	1 x 25 minutes
Five On Kirrin Island	2 x 25 minutes
Five Go Off To Camp	2 x 25 minutes
Five Get Into Trouble	2 x 25 minutes
Five Fall Into Adventure	2 x 25 minutes
Five On A Hike Together	1 x 25 minutes
Five Have A Wonderful Time	1 x 25 minutes
Five Go Down To The Sea	2 x 25 minutes
Five Go To Mystery Moor	1 x 25 minutes
Five On A Secret Trail	1 x 25 minutes
Five Go To Billycock Hill	1 x 25 minutes
Five Get Into A Fix	1 x 25 minutes
Five On Finniston Farm	1 x 25 minutes
Five Go To Demon's Rocks	2 x 25 minutes
Five Are Together Again	2 x 25 minutes

1982

Five Go Mad In Dorset A half-hour parody. A segment of *The Comic Strip*, starring Dawn French and Jennifer Saunders.

1983

Five Go Mad On Mescalin A half-hour parody. A segment of *The Comic Strip*, starring Dawn French and Jennifer Saunders.

1995-97

Zenith North series Two series, each of thirteen 25-minute episodes. The series used all 21 Famous Five novels, five of which were made into two-parters. All episodes have been released on video.

First series

Title	Running time
Five On A Treasure Island	2 x 25 minutes
Five Get Into Trouble	1 x 25 minutes
Five Go Adventuring Again	1 x 25 minutes
Five Fall Into Adventure	1 x 25 minutes
Five Go To Demon's Rocks	1 x 25 minutes
Five On Kirrin Island Again	1 x 25 minutes
Five On Finniston Farm	1 x 25 minutes
Five Go Off To Camp	1 x 25 minutes
Five Have Plenty Of Fun	1 x 25 minutes
Five On A Secret Trail	1 x 25 minutes
Five Go To Smuggler's Top	2 x 25 minutes

Second series

Title	Running time
Five Go Down To the Sea	2 x 25 minutes
Five Run Away Together	1 x 25 minutes
Five Have A Mystery To Solve	1 x 25 minutes
Five Go To Mystery Moor	1 x 25 minutes
Five On A Hike Together	1 x 25 minutes
Five Have A Wonderful Time	2 x 25 minutes
Five Go Off In A Caravan	1 x 25 minutes
Five Get Into A Fix	1 x 25 minutes
Five Are Together Again	1 x 25 minutes
Five Go To Billycock Hill	2 x 25 minutes

Appendix 7

FAMOUS FIVE ON STAGE

In 1955 Enid Blyton wrote a play featuring the Famous Five in an original story. It was staged over two Christmases in London and she helped to cast the children in the leading roles, as well as going to several of the rehearsals.

The 1990s musical was based largely on *Five Go Adventuring Again*. Three different teams of children played Anne, George, Julian and Dick in the course of the play's tour. The musical was released on video in 1997 under the title, **Smuggler's Gold**.

1955/1956
The Famous Five Staged at the Princess Theatre

1956/1957
The Famous Five Staged at the London Hippodrome

1996
The Famous Five Musical Staged at the King's Head Theatre, Islington.

1997
The Famous Five Musical Toured round the country, including performances in Bath, Oxford, Woking, Canterbury and Worthing.

Appendix 8

FINDING OUT MORE

If you want to find out more about the life and work of Enid Blyton you should look out for the following books:

Enid Blyton The Biography by Barbara Stoney
Published by Hodder & Stoughton.
The Enid Blyton Dossier by Brian Stewart and Tony Summerfield
Published by Hawk Books.
The Enid Blyton Adventure Treasury, compiled by Mary Cadogan and
Norman Wright
Published by Hodder & Stoughton

If you are a real enthusiast you might join The Enid Blyton Society which publishes a forty page magazine twice a year.

For full details of the Society, send an SAE to:
Tony Summerfield, 93 Milford Hill, Salisbury, SP1 2QL.